SWEEPING ASHLEY

NEW YORK TIMES BESTSELLING AUTHOR
EVE LANGLAIS

D1521481

PROLOGUE ~ LUCIFER

"You stink. Yes, you fucking do," the Devil crooned to his son as yet another nappy got tossed down a chute for incineration. He never left anything with bodily fluids lying around. Used tissues, sweaty clothes, everything got cleaned or eradicated, both for him and his children.

Some people out there would do anything to harm the Baphomet family. They'd die for trying, but given that Lucifer already had his hands full, he didn't need to be hunting down potential assassins, torturing them for their temerity, and making the entire event a public spectacle to curb others contemplating insubordination.

Although, he did look forward to when the dangers threatening his reign slowed down so he could test out a few new punishments he'd devised.

As to why he was the one wiping exploding asses? His wife—a word that still curled his lip. Really, the Devil being married? It went against the natural order, as did monogamy—insisted they care for their children themselves.

No nanny. Or house trolls. No robots, even. The entire child-rearing process was to be handled exclusively by family. Lucifer got the shitty job of diaper changes mostly because Gaia declared they took after him, meaning they were extra foul when things came out the back end.

Chips off the old demon they were, his young son and daughter. His pride and joy. Not yet his favorites, though. Of his four current children, he was still most fond of Muriel. But she didn't have much time for her father these days. She claimed she was busy with a kid of her own and five lovers.

Lucky cow. Stupid monogamy. It wasn't a Baphomet tradition. While he was stuck going against his nature, his eldest children were enjoying orgies.

Or at least Muriel was. He wasn't sure what the fuck was going on with Bambi.

His eldest living child, Bambi, was a proper daughter. Respected her father but sinned and fucked every chance she got. It was a miracle she'd turned out so well. He'd only gotten custody of her when her mother died. By then, she was already in awe of him, meaning he never achieved the same kind of bond with her that he had with Muriel.

He'd raised her pretty much since birth and had been a single dad for a while when her mother disappeared on them. Gaia had her reasons. He forgave her after she promised blowjobs every time she lost her temper and launched a category four or five hurricane.

Wouldn't you know they'd just had the mildest season on record?

She'd tricked him. Wily wench. And she thought she'd fooled him into agreeing to care for their children.

As if. He'd known exactly what he'd agreed to. To be honest, he was quite intrigued by his son—even if he shat and puked and cried all the time. Junior had already shown an interest in demolishing the world, his baby feet smashing the diorama Lucifer kept in his office. Building blocks went flying as thousands of hours of effort were destroyed by a Godzilla baby. Junior capped it off by swallowing one of the figurines. It eventually got shat out while Lucifer was giving the little fucker a bath.

Ah, the potential in that child. Yet it wouldn't be Junior who eventually terrified the mortal world and the realms in between. The Devil had a—

"Da!" Junior yanked on Lucifer's goatee, hard enough to pull out some hairs.

"Little bugger. It's bedtime."

"No!" Another word the not-even-knee-high terror was known to overutilize.

"Hate to break it to you, my little destroyer, but I'm in charge." For the moment, at least. The future was murky regarding how long that would last.

Lucifer huffed some smoke in the child's face, which brought a smile to Junior's lips.

"Da. Da." His eyelids drooped, and Lucifer ignored the twinge of guilt.

Yes, he'd promised Gaia that he'd rock the boy to sleep and not use his power. But the Devil had things to do. People to see. He didn't have sixty minutes to spend rocking—not to mention that hour turned into six at least, given he had a tendency to give in to snoring before his son.

No napping today.

Lucifer placed his boy in the reinforced crib with the cage on top. It only took Junior escaping once and being found in the dragon den for Gaia to agree that they needed something. The Devil's son could achieve much mischief when inspired, and this even though Luc had already restrained the child's magic. It would remain bound until he reached a certain age, and then the hormones would lead to the unlocking of it. In other words, sex would set it free. Luckily, Lucifer had a while before he had to worry about Junior coming into his power.

With his boy sleeping, he only had Jujube to deal with. Not the baby's actual name, but the one he liked best given his daughter looked like a bonbon. Pink and delicious. She still had that new baby smell he enjoyed so much. The cutest ticking bomb.

Literally. He held the most dangerous thing to the future. Killing her now would prevent so much. Avert the deaths of millions. He could save the world.

At this age, she had few defenses. It would be easy; however, Lucifer wasn't one to take the path of least resistance, especially not once he saw the potential inside her.

She would one day pose a true threat to his life and throne.

Save yourself. Don't be dumb this time. You know how this ends. Finish it now.

She blinked the longest, darkest lashes at him, and her perfect rosebud mouth stretched into a smile.

She grinned at her father.

Lucifer held her in front of him and crooned, "Who's my sweet baby girl? What a beautiful girl. Daddy's hellion." He tucked Jujube close, and she snuggled her cheek against him.

For a moment, he thought about the prophecies that spoke of her coming. The stories and predictions that he'd been collecting and hiding for millennia.

She, whose coming was foretold. And with her arrival, chaos—which wasn't necessarily a bad thing.

It had been a while since everything had devolved into pure anarchy. Ages since Hell had played freely on the mortal plane. It only ever happened when Lucifer's brother turned his back on the world.

Every so often, Elyon, the one many called God, the one true god, our Father—he truly was, of more than a few bastards. When the news came out that he was the former Antichrist's father, Elyon threw a hissy fit. Tried to start a war with Hell. Failed. Which was when his other son, who it turned out wasn't his only son, Lucifer's nephew—Jesus/Charlie—had a bit of a meltdown. He'd said fuck humanity, and with his father in tow, retreated to Heaven. Luc's advisors tried to claim that his nephew sulked.

Lucifer was more inclined to think the prat was plotting.

Which meant, a war was coming.

Fun. Fun. Fun.

Sparring with the angelic host always provided entertainment. The Devil thrived on pitting his legions against those holier-than-thou, white-winged pricks. They thought they were so fucking special because they lived in Heaven. A so-called perfect place.

Lucifer called bullshit. On the outside, it would seem ideal. Heaven with its perfect sunny days, never any clouds or rain or storms or pretty much… anything. It was the blandest place you could imagine.

Nothing changed. Ever. The food. The seasons. The people.

Bor-r-r-ing!

Lucifer had once been jealous of his brother. Why did Elyon get the perfect place, while Lucifer got cast into Hell?

For a long while, resentment simmered until he had an epiphany during an epic drug binge where he saw the truth and finally admitted: Hell suited him. He liked the sprawling madness of his circles that grew or shrank depending on the population. The wide variety of architecture. The hum of damned souls, and demons, and the rest of his people.

It was dangerous. And stressful. Exhilarating. Maddening.

Everything all the time, demanding his attention, consuming him.

But he thrived on it. The more drama, the better. And Jujube, his sweet daughter, would bring more than her fair share if she lived. If she went to war against his granddaughter Lucille, the world would be torn apart. If they joined forces, though...

They would boldly go where he and his brother had never dared to go before. In all these futures, only one thing seemed constant.

A sleeping Jujube huffed against his skin.

He murmured. "Who's going to love her mama forever and ever and never kill her?" Surely, there was a future that kept both his daughter and wife alive. Although, he'd yet to locate any out of the one hundred and one prophecies he'd located thus far. Maybe none of them would come true. After all, he'd been wrong before. He'd once thought it was Muriel who would kill Gaia, her mother.

During Muriel's youth, he'd kept them apart for as long as he could. Eventually, Muriel and her mother met. There had been a knife involved, but everyone survived. As it turned out, Muriel wasn't the one being spoken of in all those predictions. He'd known for sure the moment Jujube was born.

The baby with the longest lashes and cutest smile was the cause of the chaos.

As he laid Jujube in the crib, she woke, eyes popping wide. In their depths, he saw a dancing flame. The baby cooed and flailed her chubby fists, reaching for him. She grabbed and missed. Reached for him again.

He shook his head. "Time to sleep, tiny princess."

She scrunched up her face, readying to let out a mighty yell.

"Don't you dare," he chided.

"Ahh—"

Before it could erupt into a full-scale scream, he blew smoke. She sucked a breath in and—

Sneezed.

Achoo! The air erupted in a burst of flame.

All the hair on his face evaporated—goatee, brows, even his nostrils felt clean as a bone whistle.

He blinked.

Jujube gazed at him innocently. Smiled. Cooed. Burped and farted before going to sleep.

Very much Daddy's girl. Boy, was the world fucked.

The moment she was down, Lucifer stepped into a rip that folded time and space, to emerge in a disco hall, formerly known as the Canadian Reaper's guild, now the Hell side headquarters for Grim Dating, his most recent effort to rebuild his army of darkness.

Inside the former death guild, they processed applications by demons to go Earthside to impregnate humans. Sounded simple, and yet...it wasn't. They had to be the right kind of matches, or he'd end up with useless minions, the kind whose only use was as cannon fodder.

His sudden appearance in the matchmaking agency led to stuttering in the music before it stalled completely. The dancing lights stilled, and all the eyes in the place turned to him.

Not a word was said.

Not a single knee bent.

No head bowed.

The insolence staggered, and Lucifer might have smitten them all if his eldest living daughter hadn't appeared and trilled, "On your knees, minions. How dare you not honor my father, your master, the greatest Dark Lord we've ever known."

He wouldn't quibble about the fact that he was the only Dark Lord they'd ever known. You couldn't replace greatness. His other daughter, Muriel, had done it once when he was on a mental health vacation, and she just about went mad.

There was haste to the obeisance that followed, and more than a few kicks by his usually better-tempered daughter. Look at her, demanding respect instead of fucking for favors.

She'd changed, and not just her demeanor.

"Bambi, you are looking…"—he eyed her business suit—"more covered than usual."

"Do you like?" She twirled as she neared, showing off the trim yet severe cut to her skirt and blouse. Her hair was pulled back in a tight chignon. Her lips, though, just as ruby red as ever.

"Let me guess, you're trying to tempt a married Christian man."

"Really, Father." She tittered. "That's so nineteen eighties. I'm a modern woman now. I don't need a man to complete me."

"Since when?" he blurted. His eldest daughter was a real pride and joy when it came to living up to the family name.

"Since I realized that men are scum. Women, too, just so you don't think they get a free pass. I've had countless lovers, and do you know that not one, not a single one, wanted me for my brains?"

"I have a few zombies in the abandoned garden you can play with if it means that much to you."

Wrong answer. Which he knew before he said it, but the roll of her eyes did amuse.

"I am tired of being wanted only for my body. I want to be respected."

"You should do what Muriel does then and chop off a few heads," Lucifer suggested. Nothing said, *"don't piss me off"* like a pile of bodies missing parts.

"I said respect, not fear."

"Respect only comes because they're afraid. Strength is what matters."

"My staff isn't scared of me." She swept a hand to encompass the people busy working, paperwork mostly, processing demonic applications to be matched with a human Earthside. So many of his denizens volunteered to fuck and impregnate for the good of his kingdom.

"Without respect, comes mutiny. Trust me, I've seen it." Over and over again. Lucifer had lived through just about every scenario. Even one where he thought Gaia had died. That Ice Age lasted a long time.

"You do you. I'll do me," his daughter said pertly.

"Sounds like a recipe for masturbation."

"Did you come for a reason?" Bambi snapped. Since when did she use that tone of voice with him?

"Don't get sassy with me. Remember who gave you this job."

For a second, fire flashed in her gaze. What had gotten into his once docile and slutty daughter? Or was that the problem? "When was the last time you got laid?"

"None of your business."

Both his brows shot up. "Who are you, and what have you done with my daughter?"

She looked less than impressed at his rather hilarious joke.

"Just like a man to underestimate my worth." She lifted her chin. "For your information, I've been working my ass off. You apparently didn't notice; business is booming."

"How well are we booming?" Lucifer asked.

"We're now up to three dozen confirmed pregnancies. More than half of them definitely present demonic traits."

"And what of the trouble I heard about?"

"We had to take one of the mothers into custody because she set up an appointment to abort when she saw the ultrasound."

"Damned modern technology." Back in the day, the baby would have been born with its tail and left in the woods. So much easier to snatch. Now, the parents wanted to keep them, cut off their tails and stubby wings, file their horns.

He missed the olden days when the arrival of a new minion involved presenting it to the Devil and dancing naked by the light of the moon. It seemed like an eternity since he'd been worshiped on Halloween by witches worldwide. Those had been some of his best orgies. His wife had put the hammer down on that particular fun.

According to Gaia, the only naked person he could throw money at and slobber over was his wife. Who currently had no interest in taking care of her poor, beleaguered husband. Kept whining she'd had a baby and was tired.

She wasn't the only one. Why he'd been yanking off on his own for weeks now. It was cruel and avoidable. If only she'd put his needs above hers. Alas, instead of sex, he had to be understanding, and letting her sleep later, taking the babies out so she could have private time. He deserved a medal for—

"Hello, still here!" Bambi snapped her fingers.

He blew out a breath. "Apparently. Don't you have a job to do?"

"I am doing my job. You, on the other hand, have been slacking."

"Impossible since I delegate everything to outrageously paid assistants." He had a veritable army of people under him, who had even more working for them.

"And they do a fine job. But as you well know, a few cases require your unique intervention."

"Must I do everything?" he lamented.

"You're so hard done by. Yadda. Yadda. Can we hurry it up to the part where you agree to handle Ashley Dust?"

"That name, it's familiar." He rubbed his chin, lying just to irritate his daughter.

"Because she's one of your special cases. A witch by your grace, not birth."

"I didn't make many of those." Not since Morgana had spurned him for that Lancelot fellow. He'd had a good chuckle when he heard that Morgana had found her lover with Guinevere.

Bambi tapped a folder that a lovely bright red demoness handed her. "Do you recognize the name Ashley Dust? She's a witch, turned in her late teens, currently hitting her mid-thirties."

He snapped his fingers. "Ah, yes. Ashley. A clean freak if I recall, at least given the last time I saw her."

Which he now avoided. It had been a while since his last visit.

It would have seemed an oxymoron to have a sorceress so obsessed with cleanliness. And yet, that very trait made Ashley Dust one of his most wicked minions on Earth. Not the wickedest, though. That still belonged to Evangeline, who was on her way to popping out another warlock/shifter hybrid. If she and her mate kept at it, Lucifer might one day field a legion of them.

"Would you pay attention!" Bambi snapped, showing some temper.

He pursed his lips, and smoke curled from a nostril. "Is your corset wound too tight? Because you are in a *hangry* mood." Probably one of his favorite new words.

"I need you to remind a few of your minions about their contracts. Those that promise their first-born in return for their powers."

"That Rumpelstiltskin always got the credit for using that as a condition, but where do you think he got the idea?" Lucifer declared, jamming a finger in the air. "Me!"

"Oh, for fuck's sake, not with the whining about Rumple again. He got the credit for that schtick. Get over it."

"*You* get over it," he mumbled.

"If you're done moping, you need to call in a few of those baby-making contracts."

"Can we start with someone other than Ashley?" he asked, trying not to whine.

"What's wrong? Are you afraid of a clean and proper witch?"

Admit his terror? Never. "Just wondering if we shouldn't start with someone more likely to get laid."

"Are you saying a witch you made, one who serves you and follows your gospel, doesn't have sex?"

"When you say it like that, it sounds super bad."

"Because it is. She's defying you. Look at her… take, take, taking what you gave. But has she given back?"

"Well, she does bounty hunt for me."

"She's paid to do that!" Bambi boomed, leaning close. "What has she done for Hell? For her Dark Lord?"

A good question. It was time that Ashley, his second-most-terrifying witch, did her part to support the legion.

But he couldn't do this alone. This was a job for Grim Dating.

1

THE MAN WEARING the hooded sweater, with his hands jammed into his pockets, sauntered down the street without a care in the world. He even whistled. He wanted her to know that he followed.

Ashley crossed the road to the other side, tucking her coat tight, keeping her head down. In making herself small, she'd only made herself a bigger target.

The steps neared and kept pace as she passed from one block to the next, lit only by scattered streetlights that only barely lifted the shadows. This time of night, no one else wandered. Windows were dark. No cars prowled the streets.

The man following Ashley waited until she was level with an alley before he rushed her. Running at her, he hissed with malicious intent, "Come quietly, or I will hurt you."

"Where do you want me to go?"

He'd chosen the alley for a reason. He knew the electronic code to punch in and unlock the metal door cemented into the brick wall. He grabbed her by the upper arm and yanked her inside.

She spared a quick glance, noticing that they were in a vast space, mostly empty, only a few crates lying around.

"What is this place?"

"Quiet. Or I'll gag you with something to make you shut up."

"Are you alone?"

"Not anymore." He leered, his teeth a jagged, black-and-yellow mess.

Revolting. "Haven't you heard of a toothbrush?" She wagged her fingers and murmured a chant, more of a low hum, the noise a spider makes as it spins some web. In her case, she spun magic, spooling it out to wrap around her attacker. She twirled him in a binding cocoon of power until the only thing he could move were his eyes. Not exactly an ideal situation for him. Ashely would know. She'd once been bound in much the same fashion. On her fifteenth birthday, she was to be the virgin sacrifice offered during a blood moon, gifting her parents and the cult they ran with untold power.

Just one problem. Having heard of their decision to spill her blood, Ashley had decided to ruin it. She gave her virginity to Herman Juxtapose, which canceled out her ability to be offered up. It was kind of amusing that her parents and their cult friends had spent years grooming her for that moment, and she managed to ruin it in thirty-four seconds.

A mumble of protest from behind the tight gag drew her attention. Her captive tried to wiggle free.

"I wouldn't bother. I learned the Shibari Magical Knot pattern from an expert." She'd had extensive studies when it came to the magical arts.

The body thrashed and mumbled some more.

A frowned creased her brow for only a moment. She smoothed it quickly. Wouldn't want to encourage wrinkles. "That is quite enough," she intoned in a soft yet firm voice. "While I applaud your impatience in wanting to turn yourself in to the proper authorities, it will have to wait until I am done with my lunch."

She drew out a cloth from her pocket and set it on a crate, the surface rose under the fabric to just the right height.

The hanging body complained some more.

"Did you know," she said, pulling out a small tripod that stretched as it snapped into shape, forming a stool, "that dietary experts recommend eating at the same time every day so as to keep our body humors in balance?"

Her captive, Bracuus Notail, escaped resident of Hell, glared.

"Perhaps had you followed a more cohesive eating pattern, you wouldn't have gotten into trouble."

His eyes widened in derision, and Bracuus snorted from behind the gag. A criminal through and through, who couldn't grasp the bad life choices he'd made—starting with skipping breakfast she'd wager. To compound his ill manners, he seemed intent on ruining her appetite.

As if she'd let that happen.

She flicked her fingers, and the bound Bracuus lifted from the floor and flipped upside down. She lifted him high above, dangling him from the rafters. Bracuus might be a demon, but on the Earth plane, they were susceptible to harm.

She pulled out her Bento box containing her lunch, everything packed in its little compartment. No junk food for her. She retrieved her napkin-wrapped utensils. Laid everything out and readied to eat.

Heard some whining from above. She twirled her hand and let Bracuus plunge a few feet.

Things got quiet after that. Perched on her stool, she ate her rice, then her protein, followed by her fruit. While daintily eating her berries, she occasionally flicked her fingers, spinning her prey lest he become complacent.

She drank from the water bottle she'd filled just that morning.

When done, she packed her things away inside her pocket that actually existed on a different plane. It had cost her more than she liked at a bazaar in Jersey, but it proved handy.

Once she'd tidied her things, she glanced around the warehouse and grimaced. It never failed. Those skirting the law always chose to hide themselves in the dirtiest locales. She'd never understand why, though. Just because they owned an evil gene didn't mean they needed to live like pigs.

Look at her. A witch in the service of the Dark Lord, and you could eat off every single floor in her house.

Pity she didn't get more choice in which jobs she was assigned. It would have been nice to have the liberty of selecting more sanitary conditions. However, she comforted herself that each misbehaving bounty taken into custody cleaned up her city—and the money was good.

Glancing down, she noticed a speck of dirt on her white slacks. That wouldn't do. She flicked it with magic, then, using a magical tether, began dragging her prey behind her. She'd drop him off at the

OAB—Office for Abnormal Beings—on Fourth Street, then head to the salon for a pedicure.

A plan ruined as a familiar smell stopped her. Brimstone could only mean one person.

Ashely turned and arched a brow. "*You*. Long time, no see."

The Devil, his hair trimmed short and hinting of silver at the temples, scowled. "I see you are still disrespecting me."

Her lips curved. "If you wanted respect, you would shave regularly and wear the right clothes."

"What's wrong with my outfit?" he blustered.

She eyed him. His green pinstriped suit. The yellow shirt, the flamingo tie, and matching socks peeking at his ankles. His spats were green. "Did you dress yourself in the dark?"

Lucifer huffed, smoke curling from his nostrils. "I didn't come here for criticism."

"Obviously you did, or you'd have dressed better. I assume you're here for my target." She yanked the bound demon close.

Lucifer grumbled. "Bracuus! Again! No going to jail this time. Straight to the latrines for you." He pointed, and her target was gone.

She frowned. "This still better count at the OAB." Only confirmed captures got the bonuses. "I've got my eye on a new Dyson vacuum. You should think about getting one. And a new dry cleaner."

"My creases are perfect!" Lucifer huffed.

"If you say so." She crossed her arms. "Are we done?"

"No."

"Then can you get to the reason you're interfering with my evening?" She hadn't seen the Devil in years. Not since his relationship with Mother Nature meant no more naked bonfires. No more orgies—not that Ashley participated. All that icky sweat and body fluids. Gross.

"I've come to collect on the terms of our contract. Namely, it's time for you to give me your firstborn child."

Ashley blinked innocently at the Devil. "Excuse me?"

"Section eight, paragraph B." The Devil pulled out the scroll with the original contract. It spun out, several feet in length with tight, inked writing—and her signature in blood at the bottom. The Dark Lord pointed.

But she didn't need to look. She knew which clause he spoke of. The one she never planned to fulfill.

"Afraid I don't have a child to give you."

"Then make one."

"Would you accept a golem?"

"No!" the Dark Lord exclaimed. "Make a baby."

"With who? I'm not in a relationship."

"Who says you need to be? Just have sex. Preferably with a citizen of my kingdom." He smiled with a few too many teeth.

"I'd rather not. Have a child, that is." Slobbery, dirty things. She couldn't help grimacing.

"Do you like being alive?"

"You can't kill me for refusing. The contract says I will give you a child or be sent to Hell when I die."

"Exactly."

"Which I accept. I'll see you in Hell when I'm dead."

"If you insist." Fire formed in his hand, and she gasped.

"You'd murder me?"

"Without a second thought. I'm the Devil. The one you signed a contract with, promising me a child."

She stalled. "To do what with exactly? Eat?"

He recoiled. "What kind of savage are you? Of course, not for eating."

"Then why do you want a baby from me?"

"Because the Devil can't have too many minions. Dark times are coming. Dark, dark times that will require a legion like we haven't seen since Heaven and Hell last went to war."

"Can't I just donate some eggs to your cause?"

"No!" he huffed. "The baby has gotta be baked in your witchy oven for it to be any good."

She sighed. "Do you know what kind of mess a pregnancy would make of my body and routine?"

"I do." The Devil grimaced. "I swear my children are trying to break the record for who can puke on me the most. The boy has almost caught up to my most impressive streak."

"Way to sell it. Do I have to?" The very idea of something spitting and puking on her… She shuddered. Raising kids was something the less tidy chose to do.

"Yes, you have to. Unless you're ready to give up your witchy powers and become a regular damned soul in Hell."

Give up the magic? Die while she was still young? Perish the thought. "I'll need some time to find a compatible partner."

"You've had twenty years. You're thirty-five, Ashley, not getting any younger."

"Thanks for the reminder."

"I don't usually like the truth. However, in this case, it's really not in your favor. Which is why we need to speed up the process. You need to be fucking someone pronto. Lucky for you, I can help."

"I thought Mother Nature put her foot down on your extra-marital activities."

"She did." The Devil scowled. "Which is why you'll be relying on Grim Dating to find you an acceptable partner."

She frowned. "You're going to set me up with an agency?"

"Not just any dating place. Mine." He flicked out the company card, and she snared it. Ashley raised her brows at the cartoon image of a reaper stabbing a heart with its scythe.

"Kind of macabre."

"My marketing team assured me its edgy. And it suits the business. After all, who else is so well-suited to deal with demons and vampires and even werewolves than the reapers."

"Meaning you're going to set me up with weirdos."

"You'll never know because they'll be wearing human glamours. Maybe I should give you one, too." Lucifer eyeballed her.

"Nothing wrong with my outfit," she huffed.

"Says you. All white? Really? You'd be more attractive with some color. Maybe fewer layers. You keep hiding your shape, and you shouldn't. You have lovely curves and—"

Crack.

The thunder overhead stopped whatever perverted compliment the Devil planned to pay. He scowled at the sky. "Calm your tits."

"Excuse me?" Ashley exclaimed.

"Not you. The wife. Thinks I'm flirting with

everyone on account of her hormones going fucking wild since the baby."

Boom.

"See what I mean?" The Devil shrugged.

"Tell her she has nothing to worry about. I am not interested. At all."

The clouds broke apart enough that the moon emerged and shone on her.

The Devil didn't look happy. "It's because I look like I'm married with children, isn't it? I'm unattractive to the opposite sex. I have a dad bod now. I am ruined because of parenthood." He started going off again, and she headed him off.

"This Grim Dating service… How effective is it in finding compatible matches?"

"Extremely. Trust me. The people working there are experts."

As it turned out, they were experts at getting it wrong.

2

A WRONG TURN added a few minutes to Derrick's commute. But he didn't mind. Wind in his face. Rumbling beast between his thighs. A belly full of strudel, bacon, and a banana smoothie.

He loved living on the mortal plane.

Arriving at his place of business, he parked his motorcycle out front. Despite the rules against it, he used a magical amulet he'd bought from a wizard to keep it hidden. Damned parking enforcement loved giving him tickets. And he knew he'd been caught on those streetlight cameras a few times. He felt bad for the guy whose license plate he'd copied. Poor fucker was in for a surprise when he went to renew.

Derrick strode into the building, all chrome and glass, super modern and gleaming. It housed Grim Dating. Not your average dating service. It was managed by Lucifer's daughter, Bambi, and had the Dark Lord taking a keen interest. Those working for it were all former members of the Canadian Reaper Guild. One of the most boring guilds to belong to. Canadians just didn't die all that much. Especially since they'd passed those distracted driving laws. The government coddled its citizens, wrapping them in many laws to keep them safe.

The lack of deaths meant the reapers for the Canadian guild had nothing to do.

But that was before. Now, they had the interesting task of acting like pimps. Or, as they were taught to say, *facilitators for the introduction of compatible beings*. The end goal being hook up as many Hell minions as possible with humans to make babies. Lots and lots of offspring to grow Lucifer's legions. It made Derrick glad that he'd had a certain clause put into his contract before he went into the Reaping field.

As he walked in, his cape swirled, a black cloud that snapped proudly, but a trait only others like him could see. It was a status symbol, a uniform of sorts. All the reapers—ahem, introduction facilitators— wore them. Imbued with magic only Lucifer truly understood. It was how Derrick traveled quickly from place to place. It also gave him special powers.

It did not, however, stop him from being late just about every day.

As soon as he walked in, Malcolm at the reception desk lifted his hooded head. "Derrick. About time. The boss has been asking for you."

"Shit." He glanced at his watch. Already late twenty minutes, it wouldn't matter if he took four more to stop on the second floor to grab coffee, two mugs of it.

He held it out as a peace offering the moment he entered the boss's reception area.

Dressed in the only red robe of the bunch, Posie, former human, the big boss's girlfriend and now the newly anointed Lady Cupid, arched a brow. "Is that coffee supposed to make me overlook the fact you're almost an hour late?"

"Am I? I got waylaid on my way here." By more than a few of the women. He grinned, the same one he used to get Kayla to help with his paperwork, and for Betty to help him make a fresh pot of coffee. "Would it help if I said I stole Medusa's Danish?" He flourished the paper bag with the bakery logo on it.

Posie inclined her head. "You know Medusa is going to flip when she realizes it's gone."

"Yeah."

Given the boss's girlfriend didn't like the serpent-haired receptionist, she accepted his offering, but still asked, "What's your excuse for being late this time?"

"My bike died on the way in to work." He'd been

rebuilding it in his spare time, and still had a few tweaks to make.

"Are you sure it's not a lady friend keeping you up late?"

He snorted. "You're the only lady I know." The women he usually hung with—and fucked—weren't the types to talk politely or dress conservatively.

"Still not interested in settling down?" she asked.

"No!" A tad too vehemently perhaps.

Posie smirked. "You sound just like Brody." With the unspoken being, *"look what happened to him."* Once upon a time, Brody Reaper, the guild commander, had been as celibate as could be. Then, he met a human.

"I hear you two are planning to tie the knot."

"He's insisting. He's old school like that," she grumbled but still appeared rather pleased.

"Better you than me." He winked. "Speaking of whom, I hear the boss wants to see me."

"You don't say? He's been waiting for you to show for an hour. Close the door behind you so I don't have to listen to the yelling," she said before digging into the Danish, ignoring the bellows outside the office as Medusa noticed the missing pastry.

Derrick sauntered into the commander's office. "You called for me, boss?

"I did, you lackwit. Would it kill you to actually

show up when you're supposed to?" Brody sat behind his desk, a massive affair with a second chair suddenly filled with his girlfriend. Posie had finished the sweet but brought the coffee.

"None for me?" Brody asked as he eyed it.

"Don't look at me. Your minion was the one bribing me with treats."

That turned a smoldering glare Derrick's way. "Are you flirting with my fiancée?"

"Never, Boss. If you want, I'll get you a coffee and steal you a donut, too."

"Maybe next time. Right now, we have a job for you."

"Did we get another runner?" While Derrick acted as a facilitator most days, he was sometimes called upon as a bounty hunter if they had a demon that misbehaved, which could vary from: got too rough on a date, didn't report in, or tried to start the apocalypse—it had only taken one zombie bite the last time.

"Not exactly. It's a special kind of case. Here, see for yourself." Brody slid the folder across the desk, and Derrick snared it, flipped through the pages, and frowned.

"I'm confused. This file is about a human. Since when do we need to collect them to return to Hell?"

"We don't. Read a bit further, and you'll see she's

not just a regular ol' human. She's a witch. One of Dark Lord's handmaidens."

"So, she's got rank. Not sure why you're giving this to me. Isn't this Marella's casefile?" Her signature was all over it. Page after page of failed matches.

It was Posie who replied. "Marella quit. Claims the witch is impossible to please."

He thumbed her file. "I see she's had a series of unsuccessful dates. Maybe she's just a b—"

The word began to form, and Posie narrowed her gaze.

"—bashful kind of girl, who takes time to get to know."

"Nice catch, but you can say it. She's definitely a bitch." Brody grunted as Posie elbowed him. He exclaimed, "What? Just saying it like it is. The woman is a bit of a nut job."

"More like a clean freak," was Posie's grudging admission. "A prim and proper one at that."

Derrick took a moment to digest this. "A prim and proper witch?"

Posie nodded.

"And she's one of Lucifer's handmaidens? I thought they were all sl—"

Another look had him tempering his initial word choice to, "—slovenly hags."

"She is definitely unique. And because of that, it's causing us some issues. It doesn't help that some of the potentials we could have paired her with had to be canceled because of her work with the OAB."

Office of Abnormal Beings, a sort of do-it-all office for non-humans. Things from helping them avoid detection, to being arrested and processed for drawing attention. "You'd think her being a secretary or processing agent for the OAB would be appealing." Bribe the right person, and they could get away with breaking the rules on Earth.

"It's a good thing you're cute because your sexism is showing," Posie declared. A compliment and insult all in one.

"What is she, then?"

"Try their top field bounty hunter."

"Really?" He whistled. "She must be a strong witch." Because humans weren't often a match for an AB.

"Very strong, which is why the Dark Lord is keen on having her paired with someone from Hell rather than a human."

"So why is she rejecting the choices?" he asked.

"She hasn't."

"I don't understand." Derrick pointed to her file. "She's had five meetings."

"She's actually been very accommodating. It's the males we've been sending who are cutting dates short or calling us, begging for extraction."

"Why?"

"That's what you need to find out. All we've managed to get out of them is that it won't work."

"So, you want me to do what exactly? It's not like I can make anyone like her."

"Follow her. Get a feel for why the matches are failing. How we can improve the selections."

"In other words, stalk a witch." He rolled his shoulders. "Okay." It wouldn't be the worst thing he'd ever done.

"Be very careful with this one. Lucifer insisted we give her the VIP treatment."

"Little princess, is she?"

"Hardly. Read the file."

He did, which was why he was late making it to her dinner appointment. But he had good reason.

Ms. Ashley Dust was actually born Mary Jane Manson to scummy parents who happened to admire a certain serial killer. After a name change, Klyde and Bonnie Manson started a cult in their trailer park. A cult that believed in sacrificing virgins. Male or female. They didn't gender discriminate. Nor were their own children safe.

The cult leaders only had the one daughter. Mary Jane, a serious girl with big, sad eyes in the only school photo they'd managed to unearth.

She became an orphan not long after her eighteenth birthday. Newspaper reports claimed only the children survived a fire that swept through the trailer park. But that only scratched the surface of what really happened.

The file revealed the ugly truth.

When a ritual sacrifice went awry, Mary Jane's parents had her locked away, planning vile things as punishment for their daughter. Only MJ wasn't about to die for a crazy cult. She brokered a deal with the Devil. Became one of his specially-made witches.

The first task she accomplished as his personal handmaiden? A special mission accorded to her by the Devil himself. "Bring me the souls of those who prey on the innocent." Which was essentially every adult in the trailer park, and a few teens, too.

MJ Manson did the Devil's bidding that very same night.

Derrick thumbed through the sparse images he had, one of the cult, drunken adults cavorting in front of trailers with awnings. The next image, a crime scene photo of the ashes left behind.

After that, the file went into her career for Satan. It noted the name change to Ashley Dust. For some reason, he found himself saying, "Ashes to Ashley. Dust to Dust."

He snapped her file shut. No need to read anymore. He understood the life she'd led. He'd carted souls like hers to Hell. People raised in poverty and despair. Abused. Wanting the power to stop it.

Needing revenge.

He understood it even as he'd lived the opposite life. He'd grown up with wealth and privilege, but he liked the bad-boy life. The way it made him feel. It eventually killed him, which was how he'd ended up in the Dark Lord's service.

"How do you feel about people blubbering and begging for mercy?"

"Do they deserve it?"

"Not if they've got an appointment to meet me," said by a grinning Devil.

In truth, not many actually complained once the reaper appeared to take them. Most people understood they'd led an imperfect life. It was the truly heinous that protested most, and they were a pleasure to drag off for judgment.

He tapped the witch's file. She was more interesting than expected. And given her background, complex. He needed to know more. See exactly what had scared off her potential suitors.

Bad breath? Most demons wouldn't care if the package was pretty.

A grating laugh?

Perhaps a curse no one had detected that spurned suitors?

Given he'd spent longer than expected immersed in her biography, he had to hurry if he planned to make it in time for her dinner date. Set up by Grim Dating at the last minute, it would give him a peek at his client.

Although, surely, he had time to stop for one street taco. And a churro. Make that two. He'd only be a few minutes late.

3

ASHLEY'S ANNOYANCE started with her date being late. It was already simmering, given the locale. The restaurant, with its dingy lighting, couldn't hide the dirty corners. The burn marks on the cloth. She'd already decontaminated her side of the table.

The single candle flicking inside a squat, smudged glass didn't help the appearance of her *date.*

Physically, he was fine. Six footish, broad-shouldered, dressed in a suit. With wrinkles and the top button of his shirt undone. His hair was reasonably clean-cut. But his gaze kept lingering on her chest area as if he could see through her high-necked blouse. The brazenness of his stare irritated.

She snapped her fingers. "My face is here."

"Are you still talking?" He sighed. "I thought the

whole hooking up thing was supposed to be about eating food, having sex, and then maybe sex again."

"Before we get to the donation of your sperm, ground rules must be laid down."

"Fine. We can talk about them after I get back from the bathroom." He left the table and didn't return. The waiter did, and sheepishly said, "Your date left. But he paid first. Said he'd rather throw himself on consecrated ground than finish the meal."

"I tell you. Men these days just can't handle a real lady." She sniffed as she gathered her coat and purse.

She exited the restaurant, her sensible pumps clicking on the sidewalk. This was the third runaway this week. It was possibly time for her to return to the Grim Dating offices and request that they tweak her profile because, obviously, something in their system wasn't working.

It should not be this difficult to get pregnant. And no, she refused to shoulder any of the blame. She wasn't about to carry the fetus of just any male in her belly. If she was going to suffer for nine months and deal with the messiness of birth, then by all that was unholy, her child would be the most perfect thing ever created!

"Someone should have told me playing hard to get was your thing," growled a voice, a moment before someone grabbed her arm and yanked her into an alley.

Shock dropped her jaw. She blinked at her date, the same one who'd walked out not fifteen minutes earlier. "Excuse me. What do you think you're doing?" She glanced at her white coat and the handprint left on the sleeve.

"It hit me as I left that you were doing it on purpose. Playing tough and bitchy. But really, it's because you're submissive inside, and you just want a man to dominate you. Show you who's master." He thrust his hips in her direction.

She rolled her eyes. "You are delusional. I have no interest in you. Now, or ever."

"No one rejects me." This time when he reached for her, she sidestepped so he missed.

The Dark Lord save her from horny half-demons. "You might want to rethink your choices right now."

"I choose you to be my slut for the night. Don't worry, I'll make sure you don't remember a thing." Spoken with a leer. He stared at her. "You are getting very sleepy."

She crossed her arms and tapped her foot.

"Very tired. Your eyes want to shut."

Her lips pursed.

The demi-demon, who was supposedly part incubus, began to look confused. But before she could haul his ass in for unlicensed glamouring, someone interrupted.

"Step away from the lady, asshole."

Ashley half turned her head to see the newcomer. He wore jeans, a leather jacket, unlaced combat boots, and a violent attitude.

"Mind your business, reaper. This is a sanctioned date."

"Doesn't look like it's going well," said the gang-member-looking guy as he stepped closer.

"The slut knows me. Playing hard to get is her thing."

"No means no," said the stranger, thumbs hooked in the loops of his pants. An idiot with a hero complex.

"While I'm sure you're trying to do the right thing, you can move along. I'm capable of ensuring this cretin understands that a woman has a right to decide who touches her body," Ashley said with a tilt of her chin. She didn't need a man coming to her aid.

"A lady shouldn't have to deal with this kind of crassness."

At least the stranger recognized her class. Still… "I assure you, I am used to dealing with such filth on an almost daily basis." She returned her glare to her date. "The OAB will want to have words with you."

The demi-demon shrank two sizes. "Fuck me. You're with the OAB? But you're so….so…human-looking." The incredulity in his tone didn't surprise her. She actually welcomed it because it meant that her years of hard work to achieve her current state had worked. She'd fought the odds and had beaten them. Now, if only people would recognize that instead of laughing—which was usually their secondary reaction when they realized what she was.

"The OAB will have to get in line. I've got first dibs." The stranger shrugged.

"And you are?"

"Derrick." For a moment, the biker guy let his cloak show, a swirl of black at his back.

"A reaper?" Her lip curled. "As the Dark Lord's personal handmaiden, I outrank you." Her gaze returned to her date. "As Satan's representative on Earth, you are under arrest."

"Like hell, I am." The demi-demon did the one thing guaranteed to stop her in her tracks. He spat. A vast string of spittle filled with germs. Gross.

She froze when she wasn't able to shield quickly enough against it. Long enough that the jerk made it out of the alley, leaving her alone with Derrick Reaper, who watched the incubus flee before eyeing her.

"Are you okay?"

"No. How utterly disgusting." She used magic to sluice the phlegm from her coat. Then pulled a bottle of enhanced sanitizer from her purse. She offered it to the stranger to be polite.

"I'm fine." He waved her off with a gloved hand.

Now it should be noted that she thought everyone should wear gloves. She always had a pair so her skin never directly touched anything that might be germ-infested. However, when a man wore gloves and happened to be in an alley alone with a woman at night... Perhaps she'd still be making an arrest. Reapers weren't above the law. If he tried anything...

She sanitized herself, and still, he stood there.

"Was there something else?" she asked tartly.

"I'm Derrick."

"So you said. I should add that I don't care what your name is. But I will offer a word of advice. In the future, might I suggest you wait and see if a lady is in need of aid before interfering?"

"Most people would call my actions gentlemanly."

"Or misogynistic because of the assumption I couldn't care for myself."

"I am beginning to see the problem," he muttered.

She arched a brow. "The only problem is your patriarchal involvement in something that didn't concern you. Now, if you don't mind. It's been a most irritating evening."

But, apparently, he wasn't ready to leave her alone. He kept close as she left the alley for the sidewalk.

"That guy was your dinner date." Stated more than asked.

"Unfortunately."

"I apologize for his actions. We never would have approved him on the roster had we known about his rapist methods. Lucifer is very clear about consent. Something about the lawsuits not being worth it."

She frowned. "Why are you apologizing? And why do you even care? My dating life is none of your business."

"Actually, it is. Or are you going to pretend that you don't know what I am?"

For a moment, his shape changed, became bigger, wider, covered in a fabric swirl of shadow.

"I get that you're a reaper. Big deal. I'm not dead, meaning you and I have no business together. Or are you going to follow me around until I croak? How does it happen? Please tell me it's quick. I'm really hoping when I go that it's an asteroid that burns me to a nice, clean ash."

"You're not dying yet, Ashley Dust."

She halted. "You know who I am."

"Of course, I do. You're the reason I'm here."

She pursed her lips. "I'm confused. You just said I'm not dying."

"You're not?

"So what other reason would you have for being here?"

"I'm with Grim Dating, and I'm here to find out why you can't get laid."

4

IN RETROSPECT, he should have probably phrased that a little less crassly. Ms. Ashley Dust had a very potent magical left hook. Since it had never even occurred to him to disipate, it connected, and actually managed to whoosh all the air out of him.

He doubled over, coughing and wheezing. "Was that necessary?"

She stared at him with a cold gaze. "You're lucky that's all I did, considering you were spying on me."

"Observing," he corrected. "And I might add that you gave us permission to do so in the contract you signed when you agreed to the terms of service."

Her gaze narrowed. "Small print. I hate the damned small print. So your company gave itself an out when it comes to spying on its clients."

"Don't think of it as an invasion. We are only allowed to observe in public places."

"That doesn't make it any better. Why start stalking me now? You're the first Grim employee I've seen, and I've been on a lot of dates." She rolled her eyes.

"Which is exactly why I was assigned to your case. Given the number of fails, there is concern that your profile needs adjustment. It was thought that if I were to perhaps act as a silent observer, I could discern where our matchmaking has gone wrong."

"At least you admit it's your fault. I really wish you would do a better job because I am getting tired of meeting unfit specimens who can't handle a real lady."

"Perhaps start by not calling them specimens?" It did take some of the fun out of it.

"Here's the thing…" She paused, only for half a second.

Long enough for him to mutter, "Derrick."

She went on as if he hadn't spoken. "I'm not dating to find love. I need to make a baby."

He winced. "That's blunt."

"It's the truth. I have a contract with the Devil, and it requires certain things of me. Having a child for the Dark Lord is one of them."

"So you just need viable swimmers. Doesn't seem so hard? Or was that the problem. Did the males we set you up with not…you know?" His gaze flicked down.

She snorted. "None of them suffered erectile dysfunction, at least that I was aware of. I should add that none of the dates lasted past dessert."

"Why?"

"Because they were inadequate, and they knew it. Most of them are smart enough to not waste our time."

"What was wrong with tonight's prospect?"

"You tell me. You were the one spying."

"I got there late," he admitted sheepishly. At her arched brow, he gruffly added, "My alarm didn't go off."

He could feel the disapproval coming off her like a cold storm.

It made him want to tuck her under his cloak and warm her up.

"My date used the same excuse for arriving two minutes after the agreed-upon hour. Ideally, he should have gotten there before me and ensured that we got the best table. But he arrived late and didn't even apologize. As you can imagine, that set a poor tone."

"Did it occur to you that he might have had a good reason?"

Only a slight twitch of her lip, yet he could swear that he heard mirth under the chill as she said, "Then he should have used it. Tardiness is a boorish trait, and I won't pass it on to my child."

"I am starting to see why he waited in the alley for revenge. Most demons don't handle rejection or criticism well."

"I said nothing. At all."

He'd wager she glared, though, which might have been worse. "How long did the dinner last?"

"Not past the appetizers, which were uninspired. No surprise, given the locale."

"You want good food, you go to A Lion's Pride Steak House. Those fuckers know their meat."

"It's cats handling food. Never in a million years."

"That much of a clean freak, eh?" He took a mental note as he reached into his pocket for his smokes. A human vice he just couldn't shake, even as a reaper. And why should he? It wasn't as if the shit could kill him anymore.

The pack went flying as she slapped it.

He shot her an incredulous look. "What. The. Fuck?"

"I don't like cigarette smoke."

"So you say something. You don't fucking slap a guy."

"You were rude in not asking. I replied in kind. Don't whine. It's not as if it hurt."

He eyed the pack of cigarettes on the ground,

then glared at her. "Again, you could have just asked me not to smoke."

"Nice won't get you to quit. How many people kick nasty habits when people around them are understanding and nice about it? They don't, because there's no incentive."

"I am beginning to see why you're a handmaiden to the Devil. You have no filter."

"It's called telling things as they are. People claim they want the truth. They don't and can't handle it when you tell them."

"Too many people lie to themselves," he agreed. "It's like the souls I collected. You'd start dragging their ass to Hell, and they'd be blubbering how they didn't deserve it. Like fuck, dickwad, you planted cameras in women's bathrooms and sold the resulting photos online. You're burning for all eternity."

She stared at him. "You get it."

"I do. People lie. And you don't." He nodded. "I can respect that."

"Not many do."

"Let's backtrack to your longest date. It lasted until what part of the meal?"

"The spot between your entrée being finished and the dessert arriving. That's when I saw it."

"Saw what?"

EVE LANGLAIS

"His sleeve slid back, and I saw he had a tattoo on his arm."

"Nothing wrong with a well-done tattoo." He had a couple that had survived his death.

"If you're in a gang. I expect more from a potential sperm donor."

He choked and really wanted a cigarette. "Um, ah, you didn't actually call him that, did you?"

"Why not? It's—"

"The truth," he finished, interrupting. "You can't be so blunt. Guys aren't always so keen about the baby thing."

"They might not be keen, but that's what they signed up for. Isn't the whole mission of your agency to facilitate fornication for the purpose of procreation to rebuild the ranks of the Dark Lord's armies?"

"Who told you that?"

She blinked. "Isn't it obvious? Grim Dating, owned by Hell Enterprises, run by the Devil's very own reapers, with lots of involvement from said Dark Overlord. That means he has a vested interest in the outcome. Since the outcome is more minions, then it's about building numbers. You only need numbers if you require armies."

"You are smart."

"Is that supposed to be followed by, *for a girl*? Or is your tone always that condescending?"

The rebuke almost heated his cheeks because he could see how she might have misconstrued. "I was just trying to say that you're smarter than the average fuckwad."

"And every time you open your mouth, you lose a few points for filthy language."

The intentional insults were cute. And obvious. "Why, Ms. Dust, are you flirting with me?"

"Most certainly not," she huffed. "Or did you miss the part where I implied your mental deficiency?"

"Exactly. You are very attracted and trying hard to not give in. It's the whole rugged thing. Makes good girls go bad all the time." He winked.

She gaped, her mouth hanging open a bit as she digested his words. Turned an interesting shade of pink.

"Your speechlessness proves my point."

"Does not," she exclaimed.

"It's okay. Although I should remind you, as an employee of Grim Dating and the one in charge of your case file, it is against company rules for us to fraternize. But…" He paused and couldn't help a grin as he said, "There isn't actually a rule against fucking.

He expected her to huff and howl at his proposal.

But she surprised him. Her lips turned up, her expression sultry as she drew near enough to put a finger on his chest. Just one. He felt it to his toes.

"You could only hope to ever fuck me," was what she whispered hotly against his mouth. Then she stepped away before bellowing, "Lucifer! We need to talk."

"Did someone say my name?" The scent of brimstone filled the air, only a moment before Lucifer himself appeared.

Derrick dropped to a knee and ducked his head. "Dark Lord."

"Rise, my humble reaper," said the benevolent King of Hell.

Derrick rose and noticed that the witch hadn't even bothered to loosen her crossed arms.

The Devil eyed her and said slowly, "How is my favorite witch?"

"We both know I'm only your second favorite. So don't you dare start. I want to change the terms of my contract."

"Can't. It's bloodclad. Can't be changed." Lucifer shrugged.

"But I can't give you a baby," she growled. "Because incompetents, like this guy,"—she jerked a thumb at Derrick—"have no idea what they're doing."

"Is Derrick not doing his job?" The Devil turned a glare on him. "I only approve of delinquency for other people. I am your Lord. You should always obey me."

"I'm doing my job fine. Your witch is just bent that she's so spectacular we've yet to find her a man."

"Don't you dare call her…" The Devil paused. "Did you call her spectacular?"

She frowned. "You don't have to lie." She turned to Lucifer. "He thinks I'm a bitch."

"I never said that, so don't put words in my mouth. You're picky, is what you are, but only because you're uptight." She wasn't the only one who could use the truth.

"Excuse me?" she huffed. A sharp breeze hinting of ozone tugged past Derrick, fluttering his cape.

"Don't you dare get insulted. Uptight is how you are."

"As opposed to dirty and unkempt?" she sassed pointedly.

"Exactly. Nothing wrong with either. But, in your case, it narrows the pool. Us dirty types aren't that picky."

"He's right, you know," the Devil claimed. "There is no one filthier than I am, and I will pretty much fuck anything."

The ground trembled.

The Devil adjusted his tie. "Not anymore, of course. Happily married."

Ashley made a moue of disgust. "I don't want to get married. Just get pregnant and get it over with."

"Why must you make it sound like a chore?"

groaned the Devil. "It's sex. Baby-making sex. The best kind. But don't tell Gaia that. I already have two in diapers, can't imagine a third," the Devil said in a hushed voice.

"I'm not that particularly fond of the act, so I'd rather just find the right candidate and get it over with."

She didn't like fucking? Impossible. Which was why Derrick said, "You just haven't been pleasured by the right guy yet."

"Are you implying you're that man?" Her tone mocked, and yet he couldn't help but picture it. Kissing her until those taut lips softened, and her lids turned languorous.

"He most certainly is!" exclaimed Lucifer. "Mind if I watch? Been a while since I've seen a master of seduction at work. Gaia made me remove the mirrors in our bedroom."

"He's not genetic material," was her cutting refusal.

"Joke's on you, Ash. I don't have any viable swimmers. So, sex with me would be just for fun." Derrick winked.

"Thanks for giving me even more reason to not waste my time." She turned away from him to fully address the Devil. "Do you see my problem? How is he supposed to help me if he doesn't get me?"

"Don't get you? I'd say at this point I have the best

fucking clue about you. And I'm probably the only one who would touch your case, given what I've discovered."

"Are you implying that I'm difficult?" she huffed.

"He would never do that!" lied Lucifer. "I'm sure he thinks you're just lovely. Tell her, Derrick."

"She likes the truth, and the truth is she has personality traits that might rub some folks raw. It just means I'm gonna have to dig deeper to find the right kind of match for her."

"You'd better find someone! Ash here is a special favorite of mine." The Devil went to pat her on the head, but a glare stayed his hand.

"I'm sure there's some—" He held in the first words that came to mind, *poor bastard to substitute* —"guy out there who will fit all her needs."

"At this point, I'd probably have more luck with a turkey baster," she grumbled.

"Oooh, totally would love to watch, but my wife,"—Lucifer grimaced—"says voyeurism is cheating."

Ashley nodded. "She's right. And for the record, having one of your goons tagging along on my dates is creepy stalkerish."

"For the last time, it's my job!" Derrick exclaimed.

"I'll bet next you're going to tell me you love your *job*."

"Are you serious? Do you really think I get off on watching a chick on dates with other dudes?"

"Don't knock it 'til you've tried it." Lucifer's brows waggled. A clap of thunder had him scowling overhead. "I never said it was you."

Another clap of thunder.

"I am not going to pretend I was celibate before we met, wench." Lucifer shook a fist at the sky.

The next bolt hit him in the crown and left a singed spot of smoking hair.

Lucifer's grimace turned fierce, and the smoke poured from his nostrils. "My most excellent presence is required elsewhere. I trust that you will find my witch a suitable broom to ride?"

"Yes, Dark Lord." Derrick dipped one knee. When he rose, the Devil was gone, and the witch was smirking.

"Yes, Dark Lord," she mimicked.

"It's called respect."

"And I'm thinking I know why you took the hood and became a reaper. To hide your brown nose."

The insult had him pushing said garment back. "More and more, I'm seeing why you'd prefer a baster. Do you ever stop insulting people?"

"Truth hurts. As does regular maintenance, apparently." She eyed him. "Ever heard of a barber?"

"Woman love my hair." He shook his shaggy mane.

"Probably because you remind them of a dog." The witch actually shuddered. "Mangy, dirty, smelly things."

He sighed. "Is there anything you *do* like?"

"Cats. They are beautiful, clean creatures."

"Listen, Ashley."

"That's Ms. Dust to you."

"Which is kind of ironic given your dislike of it."

She didn't seem as amused.

"For fuck's sake, can we just start over? Let's pretend I wasn't spying on you, and I instead contacted you for a meeting." He held out his hand. "I'm Derrick Reaper. A Grim Dating problem solver."

She saw the hand and ignored it. "Even had you approached me first, I don't know what you think spying will do to help me. I already filled out the questionnaire."

"But, sometimes, a form doesn't capture everything. I'm going to give you a more personal interview. Say, tomorrow, Three p.m. at the Grim Dating offices."

"That won't work. Some of us have a job, you know."

"Then how about tomorrow evening?"

"I was planning to stay in, given the last few nights have been failures."

He restrained the urge to throttle her. Barely. It

adrenalized him, reminded a man why he liked a woman with fire. "What if I come to see you?"

"If you must." Accompanied by a long-suffering sigh.

And then she strode out of sight in her sensible pumps, impractical white coat, and sassy attitude.

The old him, before he'd become a reaper, would have had a way of taking her down a notch or two.

New him, though…saw her as a challenge.

She didn't think he could do his job.

Ha.

He'd show her.

5

ASHLEY DID her best to forget the scruffy Derrick. She didn't hold out much hope that he'd be able to help her. And yet, he had pegged her accurately.

I am high-maintenance. With high standards. Nothing wrong with that.

But as he mentioned, it did make finding her someone compatible tricky. As a result, he planned to come here the next evening and interview her.

Why had she agreed?

She'd cancel. She didn't want him coming inside. He'd probably leave a grease stain with those dirty jeans of his. She pulled out her cellphone, along with the Grim Dating business card. She texted their primary number.

This is Ms. Dust canceling her appointment with your associate, Derrick.

Succinct. It revealed nothing.

A few minutes later, she got a confirmation. *Message received and forwarded to the appropriate party.*

Meaning they'd sent it to Derrick?

For some reason, the idea had her pacing and glancing at the wall clock. After ten. He wouldn't dare text back tonight, not this late. If he replied at all, it would be in the morning.

Ding.

A message came in from an unknown number.

Coward.

Her heart stilled. *Who is this?*

Who do you think? Let me guess, you're canceling to wash your hair.

For some reason, the caustic reply made her smile.

I'm trimming my nails too.

She saw the flashing dots showing he replied, and she stared at the screen until the words appeared.

Sounds like your evening will be pretty full. Guess we'll have to reschedule.

Guess so. Maybe next week when I'm not so busy. *Or never* was her real thought.

Maybe the dating thing wasn't for her. It might be time to look at a sperm bank. The Devil wouldn't be happy about it, but at least then she could control what she put in her body.

What are you doing right now?

Talking to you, was her sassy reply. She stared at the screen, realized he wasn't typing. She added. *And getting ready for bed.*

Another pause. Nothing.

She typed, *Goodnight* and put the phone down.

Then she let out an unladylike yodel when he said, "We really need to talk about your aversion to color."

"How did you get here?" she exclaimed because the chain on the door still hung across.

"I might be a facilitator for the introduction of compatible beings, but I've still got my reaper powers." He swung his cape, and she saw it for a moment, a swirl of darkness that almost swallowed him. Then it was Derrick again, wearing the same disreputable jeans, black steel-toe boots—scuffed and unlaced—but he'd ditched the leather jacket. He'd swapped it out for an open plaid shirt, layered over his tee.

"Wow, being able to just appear in people's houses is awfully convenient for your peeping habit."

"I don't use it to—" He shook his head. "Never mind. You're right. I use my reaper skills to secretly watch women as they brush their teeth. Nothing more erotic than that foaming mouth and the spit." He rolled his face upward and moaned.

"So funny," she said dryly, and yet, she was amused. "Why are you here?"

"Because you canceled tomorrow's appointment."

"And you just had to come over and whine in person?"

"You said to reschedule. So, I did. For right now. Would you prefer the kitchen table or the couch?"

"Make yourself at home much?" She arched a brow. "I never said you could come over tonight. I was just about to go to bed. Some of us need sleep because we work in the morning."

"If you cooperate, this won't take long."

"I'm pretty sure my contract doesn't give you permission to ambush me at home."

"Probably not. You really want to get lawyers involved or get this done? I'm sure the Devil won't mind waiting."

Her lips pursed. Lucifer wasn't known for his patience. "What do you want to know?"

"Let's begin with the things you hate."

"It would be quicker to list the things I like."

"Name your three favorite things."

It seemed an easy question, just three. Favorites. What did she really enjoy? "My house."

Not having much of a budget, she'd been forced to buy in a less-than-stellar neighborhood. It meant working extra hard to achieve and then maintain an immaculately maintained bungalow, especially given the dilapidated state of the housing all around.

"I couldn't help but notice you are the only non-condemned house on the block," he remarked.

"Makes for quiet neighbors."

"Was it cheap to buy in?"

Her lips pursed. "That's a rude question to ask."

"How is it rude? I might be interested in buying. I'm not big on apartment living and noticed the place across the street is for sale."

The very idea of him becoming her neighbor rankled. "You can't buy it."

"Why not?"

"Because I prefer those homes empty."

"Seems like it would be safer if there were more people about."

"Implying a woman can't live alone?" Spoken with a sneer.

"Thieves and shit don't care who you are, they just like to steal stuff. The more people around, the less likely it is that they'll hit you."

"They know better than to touch my house." A hint of a smile curved her lips at the reminder of what had happened to the last guy who'd tried to break in. He remained in the hospital, recovering from the mental break he'd suffered.

"Why are you afraid to have people near you?"

"I'm not afraid."

"Aren't you?" He stepped into her bubble.

She moved away. "I don't like people too close to me."

"Why?"

"Because they breathe and shed germs." She shuddered. "Haven't you heard of the three-foot rule?"

"Rules?" He snorted. "We're the Devil's minions, do we really care?"

"Those of us with human genes do."

"I'm not contagious."

Funny he should say that because when he stepped close, she heated as if feverish. No ignoring the fact that he was there. Very male. Handsome. Seemingly intelligent.

In the end, he'd just disappoint her like everyone else.

She moved to the one chair in the living room. Too small to share, forcing him to either keep standing or seat himself across from her on the couch.

He flopped across it, six-feet-something of lanky male with his boots—now resting on her white leather couch!

She finally clued in to the fact that he'd not removed his outer footwear and snapped.

"Were you raised in a barn?" She pointed her

finger, and they were zapped. A fine silt sifted down, and would require a vacuum.

"Ashes to ashes. Dust to dust." He didn't look bothered one bit as he wiggled his toes, the big one sticking out of the hole in his gray socks. Gray because he obviously didn't use bleach when he did laundry. "I can see why you chose it."

"My name has nothing to do with that stupid expression."

"Yet it suits you." He grinned as he tucked his hands behind his head. He shoved at his socks with his feet until he managed to shove them off. Where they dropped to the floor. Then, he put his large feet on the armrest to her couch.

The twitch under her eye? Could probably be solved with his murder. But did she really want blood on the white leather of her sofa?

She'd sterilize once she got rid of him. "Can we get this stupid interview over with?"

"What do you think I've been doing?"

"Goading me."

"Exactly. Best way to take a person's measure is to yank their chain. Unless they're vegan. Then just feed them cheese."

"That's wicked."

"I know." His eyes actually twinkled, and she couldn't help a little smile.

"This entire time, you've been needling me on purpose?"

"You call it needling, I call it having a conversation."

"A conversation isn't supposed to antagonize."

"I doubt that happens often with you. After all, like you said, the truth hurts."

He used her own words against her. Clever. She couldn't complain without seeming hypocritical.

"I don't see how a conversation will help. It's becoming obvious that your agency is too incompetent to find me an adequate specimen."

"You can't give up."

"Never said I was. However, I do believe it is time to take my search elsewhere."

"You're going to ditch us for a rival dating company?"

"More or less. I'm thinking somewhere with less social interaction and guaranteed results."

He stared at her for a second. "Hold on a second. Are you talking about using a sperm bank?"

"I know the Dark Lord wanted it done the more visceral method. However, after some thought, I believe having my implantation done in a sterile environment is probably best."

He blinked. "Holy shit. I just figured out what we've been doing wrong."

"You have?" she asked.

"Before you get probed and implanted, give me one more chance. I think I've got someone for you."

"Really?" For a moment, she expected him to suggest himself.

Only he whirled. "I should have thought of Terry before. I'll get it set up. Tomorrow night."

"I'm—"

"Going. Don't argue with me on this, Ash."

She pursed her lips. "What makes you think this time will be any different?"

"Because I finally see where we went wrong."

Despite knowing that she'd be disappointed, she found herself agreeing. "Fine. One more chance, and then I'm filtering for baby basters."

6

ANY PLANS he had on talking more with Ashley were dashed as she claimed it was late, and she needed to get to bed. She worked for an insurance office as the person who said no to people making claims. For some reason, he could see her doing well at it.

Ash shoved him out the front door before he could remind her that he'd teleported in. More or less. *Teleport* wasn't the exact term for what he did. Nor did he always control it. The magic of his cape allowed him to move through a netherworld, a bottomless limbo that somehow cut distances short.

Some might call it trans-dimensional. He called it ball shriveling. The nothing place knew how to make a man, even a reaper used to death, feel insignificant.

Strutting down the sidewalk, hands shoved into

his pockets, he noticed the tidiness of the place anew. While the houses all around peeled and sagged, hers possessed a defiant air that dared mold or decay to touch it. The yard sported a white picket fence, bordered by yellow tulips and a mat for wiping shoes that looked like no one ever dared. It appeared incongruous, smack dab in the neighborhood, and he wondered just how hard she needed to protect the place from vandals who surely wished to sully the pristine cleanliness of the joint.

Heck, he wanted to pull up a few shrubs, maybe plant some wildflowers just to mess with her oh-so-perfect landscaping. She thought he'd been doing it on purpose to bug her about having neighbors. Yet seeing her isolation, he couldn't help but wonder about her safety.

She was strong, but not infallible. He was well aware the weak had a tendency to gang up on those kinds of people. He stepped out of her yard and wished he'd brought his motorcycle. However, he'd followed her texting signals through the nothing place to find her.

Cell phones. Best invention ever. Made tracking people so much easier.

He swirled his cloak around him and, just like a girl with ruby red shoes, thought, *There's no place like my shithole.* He was ported to the street outside the apartment he was currently renting. A basement unit with low ceilings but free Wi-Fi from the restaurant overhead.

Walking in, he grabbed a beer and a slice of leftover pizza before using his computer to log on to the Grim Dating portal. He never worried about anyone stealing his equipment. Only the dumbest crook would want the massive monitor and the slow, chugging computer still running a DOS-based system.

Not sure what DOS is? Because it's old! Disk Operating System. Clunky. Required a bit of skill to actually use, which made it perfect for this time. Not to mention, Hell had a shit ton of the old machines kicking around. It wasn't only the damned souls that ended up in the nine circles.

Company rules forbid him from bringing paper files home, on the off chance that humans got suspicious and raided his place. He had to do his research online, using the special log-in protocols he had been assigned to keep his browsing secret. Anyone trying to spy would see him surfing porn or playing *Jill of the Jungle*, a classic.

While the pixelated character jumped and fought the game, Derrick pulled up Ashley's file to further study it. Drew the parallels between her past to the present. She was a woman who didn't want people getting close to her. Who'd lived in filthy conditions, with abuse, and now sought to control her environment.

She was highly intelligent, at least according to her school records. She showed plenty of common sense, as well. She'd appeared ballsy thus far, although how far that courage extended had yet to be tested. He'd wager that she feared almost nothing. He remembered when he'd felt the same way.

In the end, it'd killed him.

In some respects, they'd lived a similar life. Raised by parents who expected them to do as they were told, even if it wasn't in their best interests.

For her, cult parents who wanted to use her to advance their ends. In his case, Derrick had been expected to conform and advance his father's business interests.

They'd both rebelled. Derrick had joined a gang, where he thrived on the danger and drama with rival groups.

He'd expected to die young. What he didn't expect was the sorrow and regret that came with it. The realization that he'd not done anything with his life. Not left a mark. He didn't even have a child to carry on his legacy.

What legacy? His parents had disowned him. He'd led a life of violence and crime. He hadn't been a good guy in life, so imagine his surprise when he got another chance. Of sorts. Lucifer chose him to be a reaper.

And now he was a pimp.

The reminder had him pulling up Terry's file.

Super neat.

Always well dressed.

Smelled nice.

Was one of the few demons given dispensation to live more or less permanently on Earth.

Now that Derrick understood Ash better, he could see that Terry was perfect. So, why did it bug him so much?

It should have been a slam dunk. The next day, his plan unraveled. The boss lady called him into her office. Posie pointed at her computer.

"You made a mistake." She tapped the image of Terry's smiling face on the screen.

"Everything lines up."

"Except for the fact that Terry presents female."

"But chose to retain male aspects."

"Ms. Dust is attracted to men."

"Are we sure about that?" The more he thought about how she'd reacted towards him and her other dates, the more he was convinced that she subconsciously didn't like guys.

"Of all the male attitudes to have…" Posie glared. "Are you trying to convince her to use a sperm bank?"

He gaped. "How did you know about that?"

"Never you mind how I know. The fact of the matter is, she's not attracted to women. Which means, Terry won't work."

"It's too late to cancel. She's already agreed to meet Terry for dinner."

"Replace them."

"With who?"

The big boss lady drummed her fingers. "I don't know. That's the problem. None of our current roster has anyone left that might be suitable."

"Then we should tell her."

"Telling her isn't the problem." They both glanced at the floor as if they could see into Hell.

"What do you suggest we do then?" Derrick asked.

Posie sighed. "I guess we let her meet with Terry."

"Didn't you just say that wouldn't work?"

"It won't. But we need to keep the witch occupied until it's time."

"For what?"

"Fate."

He frowned. "How's waiting for Fate supposed to help."

"Because Fate will show us the way."

Really, because upon leaving the office, the only thing he could think was that he was more turned around than ever. But in good news, his bike was running, and for once, he was early, which might be why he checked out the house for sale across the street from Ashley's.

He wouldn't mind having a place with more room than his cramped basement apartment. At least that's what he told himself as he went through the rat-infested dwelling.

The place was a dump. Not worth the time it would take to rehab. He made that decision as he stood outside.

Then, since he was in the neighborhood already...he thought he might as well see if Ash needed a ride.

7

For some reason, she put more care than usual into her outfit. Not that Ashley held out much hope for her date. This time, rather than give her any details, they wanted her going in blind. No preconceived notions about how she'd dislike a man who parted his hair on the right instead of the left. She also couldn't do searches on him ahead of time to see if he had any weirds posts on social media. You could tell a lot by a person by what they posted.

Grim thought she should go in with a fresh mind and make an actual first impression based on her gut.

Her intuition said she'd hate him.

Just like she'd hated all the other guys they'd set her up with.

Was she really that difficult? Was it too much to

ask that she not want to shove a metal straw through their eye?

Better not. It would probably be messy.

Much cleaner to choke them.

"Ah, now there's a look I know and adore." The Devil appeared, a child on his shoulders, a young one with big, green eyes and a mop of dark hair that flopped. The boy clung and stared, sucking his soother.

"You honor me with your presence, but could you take off your shoes." She glanced at his feet.

The Devil shifted. "They're clean. Stolen from the casket before they buried it."

"No shoes inside." She pointed.

The Devil's shoulders slumped as he snapped his fingers and put some hairy feet, large like snowshoes with a hint of hair on the toe knuckles, dug into her carpet. The burning smell didn't bode well.

"I am barefoot, happy?"

"Ecstatic. Why are you here,"—pause—"my lord?"

Lucifer's grin held mischief. "You do the disrespect so well. No wonder you're my second favorite."

She rolled her eyes. "If I slip to third or fourth, will you go away?"

"I'll go away when you finally complete the terms of your contract. Give me a baby."

"Any baby?" she queried with a serious mien. How hard could it be to steal one?

"Such a smartass. Your baby. From your loins, to be specific."

"I'm working on it."

"Are you, Ashley?" cajoled the Devil. "You know, the process would work better if you'd stop scaring off all the potential candidates. I don't get it. You're reasonably pretty. Intelligent, too much at times, but some folks like that. Sassy. So very, very sassy. But again, not always a bad trait." The Devil rubbed his chin. "Ah, yes. I know what it is now, the problem with you. You're b—"

"Bitchy?" she supplied.

"As if I'd be so crass." Sounding highly offended, the Devil recoiled. "No, I was going to say brash, your bold nature requires someone not daunted by it. A man who can stand up to you. Yet, at the same time, you need to feel superior, to know you could slap him across the face for no reason, and he wouldn't slit your throat. That's not an easy man to find."

"You all make it sound like I'm being picky. They're the ones running away." And in the case of her last date, tried to attack her.

"Because they're not good enough for you," Lucifer exclaimed. "No one is good enough."

"I have a date tonight," she declared. "Which I am leaving for now."

"Why bother? We both know you're not interested in whoever shows up. You'd be better off staying home. Watch a movie. Relax."

"I'll make that decision myself." She went to move around the Devil, but he wasn't budging, and she wasn't ballsy enough to hip-check Satan out of the way.

"So determined to go. And fail."

"If I fail, then maybe your dating agency will be able to see where they went wrong."

"Oh, is Derrick going along with you?" the Devil asked innocently.

But she knew better. She'd slipped up. "Maybe. I don't know," she mumbled. He'd not actually said he would be shadowing her.

"The real question is, do you think he's handsome? Would you want to take a ride on his broomstick?"

"What? No!" she hotly exclaimed, her cheeks suddenly flaming.

"Lies!" Lucifer boomed. "We both know he's got some fine features. And an even better ass." The Devil winked and plucked his child from around his neck to cradle it in an arm.

"I am not interested in him like that," she retorted, perhaps a little too vehemently. "Not to mention, he's not much use, given he already said he can't procreate."

"Is that the only thing in your way?" the Devil queried, a sly expression in his gaze.

"How about the fact that I'm not interested in him? Now, if you don't mind."

"Actually, I do."

"Too bad. I have to go. I'm going to be late."

"With any luck, yes, yes, you are." The Devil winked, the boy winked too, and then they popped out of sight.

She was left staring with pinched lips at the singed footprints he left behind in her lovely white shag. Forget snowshoes, they appeared more like cloven hooves.

As she headed out the door, her phone buzzed. A text from Derrick. *Need a ride?*

She should say no. She could easily walk to where she was going, but it would take a brisk fifteen minutes, and if she missed a crossing light, she would definitely be late. Damn the Devil for interfering with her schedule.

She could accept the ride from Derrick, proving to Lucifer and herself that she had no interest in the reaper. Why waste her time with Derrick when all she needed was a man with a viable seed to sow her garden?

Given she hated playing in the dirt, that wasn't the best analogy. It made it so unappealing. Why couldn't she be like other people and just jump into sex with anyone she met?

Maybe tonight's blind date would be that man.

She should make a good impression. Arrive on time by accepting a ride.

A choice she regretted the moment she stepped outside and saw Derrick straddling a motorcycle. He wore a helmet and goggles, and a big freaking grin. "Hey, Ash. You are smokin' tonight."

Pleasure suffused her. His compliment shouldn't have mattered. "I can't ride with you," was her reply.

"Why not? It's big enough for two, and look,"—he reached into a saddlebag—"I brought a helmet for you."

A beanie flat top painted with flames. Used, she'd wager. Even if it weren't, she'd have to jam her hair inside it. Then straddle his belching bike in her white slacks and hold on tight. Fumes would cake her. She'd be a mess.

One who would get to hold on to Derrick. The very fact that she contemplated it got her feet moving.

Away from him.

He kept pace, peddling Flintstone style with his feet. "Are you that much of a neat freak that you won't get on the back?"

"I wouldn't say it's freaky. I like things done a certain way. Nothing wrong with cleanliness."

"Except life and love are usually messy."

"Then we might have a problem." She kept walking, not glancing at him but aware he remained by her side.

"Why are you afraid of a little bit of dirt and chaos?"

"I'm not afraid."

"You are."

Something almost like a breeze that she could see swirling around her legs, stopped her, and she turned to face him.

"I'm not scared." She lifted her chin.

"I know you're lying. It's because of what happened with your parents."

She pulled her lips into a line. "I don't need to be psychoanalyzed."

"Actually, you do. That's why I'm following you, remember?"

"How could I forget that I'm failing at the most basic thing—attracting someone to screw me."

"Nothing wrong with being discerning."

"If there's nothing wrong, then why must you humiliate me by watching and listening?" she exclaimed.

"So I can better serve you." The words were almost purred, and for a moment, their gazes held, awareness snapping between them.

Her lips parted. He broke the stare first and turned

away. The strange tug disappeared, and she could walk again. Ignored him until he finally lost interest.

A motor chugged, then roared as he sped ahead, leaving her to watch his back and wonder what it would be like to hang onto him. Add in some speed and exhilaration…

She gave herself a good shake. Why was she thinking about Derrick that way? She blamed Lucifer, planting the idea in her head.

Entertaining carnal ideas about her Grim Dating advisor would lead to her failing the terms of her contract with the Devil. She had to remind herself that Derrick couldn't give her a baby—but he'd probably be lots of fun. Though was a bit of pleasure worth the forfeit of her life?

It should have been an easy answer. She bit her lip and was still biting as she entered the restaurant. Given the agency had insisted on a blind date, she'd chosen the locale, the cleanest place she knew with impeccable standards.

Since she ate here often, the staff knew her and led her right to her table, which already had an occupant. She was only thirty seconds late.

How mortifying, especially since the man waiting for her was quite handsome. He wore a white shirt tucked into cream-colored pants. The crease on them was so crisp it could cut.

He was clean-shaven. Blond and blue-eyed. Square-jawed. His nose perfectly aligned, no crooked hump as if it had been broken like Derrick's.

A smile stretched his lips, and he stood at her approach. Even sketched a little bow.

"Hello. You must be Ms. Dust," he greeted. "I'm Michael Angelo. My friends call me Mike. Which I hate," said with a self-deprecating smile.

"And I'm Ashley, not to be shortened to Ash." She held out her gloved hand and saw he wore a thin leather pair, the same cream hue as his shoes.

His shake was firm, not too long or attempting to prove his strength. His scent pleasant.

He gestured. "Shall we sit?" Michael held out her chair.

She couldn't fault his manners. "Thank you," she said as she sat.

Michael tucked the chair closer to the table before seating himself across the way, not being too forward and trying to sit right beside. He continued to smile. "You're not what I expected."

"I'd say ditto, except they didn't tell me anything about you." She shrugged. "Something about me having a preconceived notion."

"I'll admit, when I heard the word *witch*, I pictured someone completely different."

"Let me guess, wearing black? Maybe some torn-up lace?"

"A warted nose at the very least," was his teasing reply.

"What do you know other than my name?" Ashley asked.

"Nothing more than you're a client of Grim Dating. I'm surprised. A beautiful woman like you should have men throwing themselves at your feet."

The compliment made her blush. "Hardly," she said with a titter. What the heck? She didn't titter.

"I find that hard to believe. Rumor has it the Dark Lord himself has a vested interest in your social life."

Her nose wrinkled. "Unfortunately."

"Why unfortunate? It's my understanding that only his most special minions have him showing interest."

"Not special at all. It's because of my contract. I owe him something. I'd rather not discuss it." Probably the first time she'd not used Lucifer's demand to scare off a date. "What about you? You don't seem like the type to need Grim Dating, either." He could have stepped off the cover of a magazine.

"I do what my lord commands me." Said with a glance upward.

Was he religious or something? And shouldn't he be looking below?

"Do you live in the city?" she asked.

"Not quite. You might say I like being above the clouds. Nothing like getting up in the morning and seeing nothing but miles of sunshine."

The waiter arrived to interrupt, filling their glasses with a wine her date had brought, a lovely vintage. There was a basket of warm bread to share, and she might have blushed when their hands touched as they both reached at once.

Their entrees were a nice complement to the conversation: eggplant parmesan for her, and squash-filled tortellini in an Alfredo sauce for him. They discussed the latest bestselling books because she liked to read. Paper, not that new electronic stuff. He went one step further and did only hard-backs. They spoke of films and places they'd seen.

He was knowledgeable, courteous, and definitely flirting in a respectful manner that didn't make her feel dirty. But she did feel guilty for some reason when she noticed Derick stalk past the hostess and come straight to their table, no helmet but still in those jeans, the thigh on one bearing a grease streak. His leather jacket was ripped and poorly patched, the whole of it spiderwebbed with age.

What was he doing? Shouldn't his stalking be clandestine?

Derrick dragged an empty chair to their table,

not bothering to remain quiet. He slammed himself in it. "Sorry, I'm late."

"What are you doing?" she exclaimed. "I'm on a date that's going well for once."

"No, you aren't," he drawled. "You going to tell her, or am I?"

Only one side of Michael's mouth curved. "You seem like you're in the mood. Go ahead."

"What's going on?" she asked.

"Mike isn't your date," Derrick declared. "Your date canceled the moment they got your name. Apparently, your reputation precedes you."

"If Michael isn't my date, then how did he know my name and that I'm a client of Grim Dating?" she asked.

"Because he's a spy for Heaven. One of their undercover angels," Derrick announced.

A snicker escaped her as she glanced at Mike. "Don't angels have wings and halos?"

Michael shrugged. "We do, but they only appear if we're in the mood to show them to humans. As for halos, those are more a Court thing. They're inconvenient when working in the field."

"Working on what?" She eyed him suspiciously. "Why are you here?"

"Because he is a troublemaker," Derrick declared. "Can't stand that his side lost the wager, and we get to keep doing our job."

Michael straightened, no longer amused. "The loss is a temporary thing. It won't be long before Grim Dating is shut down. You'll break the rules at some point and get caught. When you do…" Michael trailed off.

"You'll be there to tattle. Can't say I'm surprised to find out you're a snitch."

"I'm a servant of Heaven and the one true god. Here to ensure his wishes are being met on Earth."

"Which doesn't explain why you're here." Ashley cocked her head. "Why did you take my date's place?"

"Because I had orders to see that Grim Dating wasn't overstepping its bounds. And what better way to ensure that nothing untoward was happening than to meet with their most dissatisfied client?"

"Who told you I wasn't satisfied?" She turned an accusing stare on Derrick, who lifted his hands.

"Don't look at me. I wouldn't piss on an angel even if his wings were on fire. The lot of them are sanctimonious pricks. It's why they can't get laid."

"Neither can this witch," she declared, shoving to her feet. "I don't know what game you're both playing, but I'm done."

8

SHE STALKED OFF, leaving Derrick with an angel wearing a beatific look he wanted to punch.

"What an interesting human," opined Mike.

"Oh no, she's not." A lie, Ashley was very fascinating, and it bothered him that the angel noticed. And worse, she'd made it to dessert with him. He'd truly expected to walk in and find her finishing her meal alone. But, as usual, he ran late. After leaving her, he'd meant to park and head in to observe—ahem, spy. Only he went a block too far, saw a store he liked with a big red banner indicating a major sale. So, he shopped for a few minutes, expecting the date to be done by the time he arrived, only to see her smiling and talking with an angel of all things.

She'd never smiled like that at Derrick. It bothered him a fair bit, and he couldn't grasp why.

"What the fuck do you think you're doing?" Derrick growled.

"I was enjoying dinner until you barged in. I'm surprised to see you here. They don't have French fries on the menu. Not to mention, you're not exactly dressed for this kind of fine dining establishment." A disdainful flick of Michael's gaze over his garments had him growling.

"I'm here because Ash is a Grim Dating client."

"Ash, is it? Not Ms. Dust?" Mike drawled with an arched brow. He had supercilious down pat. "I didn't realize your agency stalked its patrons. How...invasive." The pause gave the comment a salacious twist.

"Ashley knows why I'm watching. I'm supposed to analyze how her dates are going so we can better serve her."

"Don't you mean find her a compatible bed mate? After all, it's all about making babies."

"No idea what you're talking about," he evaded. Part of the reason they could operate was because the Devil lied. Told Heaven they were just helping like-minded people fall in love. The truth was more complicated. And against the rules.

Mike knew he wasn't telling the truth. "It's actually a brilliant idea. Personally, I'd rather see demons getting with willing partners than that mess we dealt with in the fifties." Referring to the spate of possessed mothers and the subsequent problems with their pregnancies. "But you didn't hear it from me."

How had they gotten so far off topic? "You still haven't told me why you're here."

"To talk to Ms. Dust, of course."

"What does Heaven want with Ashley?"

"Who says it's Heaven that's interested?" Angels could look as sly as the next fucker, and Mike was no exception. But while some people might be ugly when they did, the man remained good-looking.

Whereas Derrick was pretty sure his scowl turned him into some kind of troll demon.

"Why are you pretending interest in her?"

"Who says it was fake?"

"Are you going to tell me the high and mighty Michael is going to break Heaven's rules to have sex with a human?"

"Who says I'd be breaking any? We might not be as prolific or short-lived as demons, but we do still need to procreate."

"Wait, you mean angels can fuck and not get cast out?" He'd heard the rumors, but hadn't been sure they were true.

"Where do you think our young come from?"

"Immaculate conception." It sounded dumb the moment it emerged from Derrick's lips.

"You cannot seriously think that." Mike's eyes widened. "I see you do. Well, let me assure you, we have to create progeny in the same manner as any other species."

"So, you can fuck?"

Mike almost winced. "Only a select few are given permission to reproduce."

"Let me guess, you're one of those guys."

"I am."

Derrick snorted. "Guess intelligence isn't a factor."

"Intellect can be taught."

"Unless you're fucking stupid to start with. What other reason were you chosen for? Other than your Ken doll looks?"

"The Lord wants his most devout to fill Heaven."

"And who are you *filling*?" He gave it an intentional crude lilt. "You giving the meat sausage to other angels?"

The wince came and went quickly as Mike said, "We cannot reproduce together. Angel with angel begets no young."

Which left demons or humans as compatible partners. "Must be hard finding someone pure enough to meet Heaven's standards to be your baby mama."

"When it comes to procreation, we only look at physical factors. Health of the mother, and that of her close relatives."

"That's mighty openminded of you. Do you have

like a ceremony to forgive Mama her sins so you can take her and the baby to Heaven?"

"Only the child is brought into the kingdom."

"You separate them?" That shocked even jaded Derrick.

"We have no choice. The mothers are sinners. The most egregious kind bearing children out of wedlock. That can't be forgiven. Therefore, they cannot pass the pearly gates."

"Sex isn't sinful if it's two consenting adults, boomer."

Michael blinked. A waste of a good joke.

Derrick leaned forward. "You are one sick fucker, which is why I'm going to warn you away from Ashley."

"A warning you are not in a position to give. She is an unattached female looking for a mate."

Derrick gaped. "You can't be serious. She's not available."

"Have you claimed her?"

"Of course, not," he sputtered.

"Are you sure, because your actions are more in line with a jealous man than a dating specialist."

As if. "The reason you can't date her is because she's contracted with us. We have to screen all her potential dates."

"Very well, then. Make me one of her suitors.

Sign me up, as they say, for your matchmaking service."

"What?" The request confused.

"Make me a Grim Dating client, if you must. And as your first order of business, arrange a second date with Ms. Dust."

"You can't just sign up to go out with her. It doesn't work like that. First off, we have to get you to fill out a huge form. Like, massive." Not really, but surely there was a way to deter Michael from this path.

"Send me the paperwork, and I'll get started."

"Once we get it, then we have to process it. Only then will we be able to find people to match you with."

"No need to do any extra work. I know exactly who I want." Mike was quite firm.

Derrick was equally so. "No."

"Why not? We're obviously compatible."

"Because you can't be our client," Derrick exclaimed, drawing attention of the patrons in the restaurant. He drew his cloak around himself and faded from their sight and memory.

Mike smiled. He knew precisely what he'd done. Smooth bastard.

"Exactly why can't I sign up for your service?" he asked.

"Isn't it obvious? You're an angel."

"And?" Again, with that elegantly arched brow. "Are you discriminating against me because of my religion?"

"Are you for fucking real?"

"Always. And I'll say it again, for a reaper who claims disinterest, you're awfully involved in Ms. Dust's affairs."

"Because I'm in charge of her happily ever after."

"Don't worry. With my skills, she'll probably have two." The wink sent Derrick diving over the table, only to crash into an empty chair. As he hit the floor, he dispersed into smoke, whirling to find his target.

Only Mike was already out of the restaurant. Cool. Confident.

Asshole.

Derrick counted to ten before following. He should remain out of reach of the angel or he might do something that would get him into trouble.

In a mood, he gunned his bike, but the speed didn't soothe. Maybe the cold beer in his apartment would.

The moment he walked in, his night got shittier.

For one, his battered, leather chair, the comfiest seat known to a reaper, was gone. In its place was a beanbag, though not just any beanbag, a pink one imprinted with red lips. And sitting in it, wearing tight jeans, stiletto boots, and a crop top?

The Devil's daughter, his other boss.

Bambi waggled her fingers. "There you are. About time you came home, I was getting bored."

"I was working."

"Yes, with that witch who won't spread those thighs. She's becoming a problem."

"How?"

"Because we're running out of guys to send to her. No one wants to go out with her. Not any normal types, at any rate," she said with a frown.

"You're exaggerating. There ain't nothing wrong with her."

"Did she hex you to say that? If you need to return to Hell for treatment, just say the word. I can have you pulled. Be advised, your pay will be docked for being an idiot who was spelled in the first place, but at least then maybe you'll start thinking with your head and not your dick."

Why did everyone keep accusing him of having the hots for the witch? "This is not because of a hard-on. It's the truth. There's nothing wrong with Ashley."

"Now I know you're lying."

"I'm not. I mean, sure, she's a bit prickly and anal about some stuff."

"I doubt anything goes up that tight ass," Bambi muttered.

"But it's only because it's how she controls her environment."

"Which is blah blah blah for she has issues. Which means it just might work," she muttered mysteriously.

"What will work?"

"Your witch and our newest client. They might be perfect for each other and solve two problems at once."

"What the fuck are you talking about?"

"I'm talking about the fact that Heaven sent us an emissary. They want to use our services to facilitate meetings between angels and humans."

"What? You told them to fuck off, right? Weren't they the ones who tried to shut us down?"

"They did. But they lost that bet, and now they've decided to cash in. Apparently, we're not the only ones dealing with reduced birth rates. Our first angel has signed up with a special request."

"Fucking Michael," Derrick spat.

"Is that his name?" She shrugged. "All I know is Heaven is checking us out, and Father said to go for it. Charge 'em a soul's arm and a leg, and the problem of who to pair Ashley with is handled."

"Her having an angel baby won't exactly fix things with Lucifer."

"Actually, her contract says she just needs to make a baby, it doesn't say if that baby needs to be part demon or not."

"You can't set Ashley up with Mike."

"Why not?"

"Because."

Bambi rolled her eyes. "Oh, fuck me, don't tell me you have a thing for her."

"I don't."

"You do, and yet you shouldn't because you of all people will get her into trouble if she doesn't give my daddy what he wants."

"I understand that—"

She interrupted. "Good. Because the date is happening."

"Fine," he snapped. "But don't complain to me when it doesn't work out."

An angel and a witch?

It would never happen, and because he was convinced it wouldn't even make it past the appetizers, he showed up early for her next date, got a prime spot for spying—erm...observing.

9

L<small>EAVING</small> the restaurant the night before, Ashley decided it was time to swear off men.

And angels.

And reapers.

This whole baby-making business was getting much too complicated. She just wanted no-strings-attached sperm.

Which was why the next day, she sent in a formal email, terminating her contract with Grim Dating. The moment she hit send, she set up appointments with sperm banks. No point in delaying it. Surely someone, somewhere, had some swimmers she could buy.

The email to Grim Dating bounced back first. Then the appointments for fertilization were canceled.

The moment she smelled brimstone, she sighed. "You again? What do you want now?"

The Devil stepped into her kitchen from nowhere, wearing a tennis outfit of short red shorts and a tight scarlet top. The headband imprinted with ducks matched the cuffs on his wrist. The tall black boots were a touch different. "Just checking on how things are going."

"I'm not pregnant, if that's what you're asking."

"Neither is my wife, but in her case, that is cause for joy. And sorrow since the reason we're not even panicked about the possibility is because I'm not getting any. So what if she squeezed out a watermelon from her snatch? That's nothing compared to me," he boasted.

"Maybe you should get that checked. That much blood loss to your brain at once could be dangerous."

"Ha. Ha. So clever. Not." The Devil turned serious. "Exactly what do you think you're doing?"

"I'm doing your bidding."

"By using frozen jizz?"

"To get pregnant and fulfill the terms of my contract."

"I want you to make me a baby. Not have some stranger squirt juice into your cervix."

"I'm pretty sure it's more complicated than that."

"Doesn't matter if it is. I won't have it." The Devil roared, and her house shook. "In order for the powers to be passed on to the fetus, it must happen in person. In the flesh. Naked, doing the horizontal or upside-down tango. Doesn't fucking matter so long as you're taking it in the pie instead of the butt."

The crudity of it made her crave a hot shower and a long-handled stiff brush. "The contract doesn't specify it has to be made that way."

"Well, I'm specifying it now," growled Lucifer, the huff of his smoky breath making her shiver.

"I tried but your dating company couldn't find me someone appropriate."

"All that's about to change. We've found your match with some help from me and my friends above." He cast a glance skyward before grinning at her. "I hear you had dinner with an angel last night."

"Pretty sure his wings are tarnished, given he lied to me."

"Did he? Or did he merely choose not to reveal the truth?"

"It's the same thing," she argued.

"On a matter of point, no it isn't. I should know about loopholes, after all, all magic and contracts have them, some tighter than others."

"I'm not interested in dating an angel. Or have you forgotten they play for the other team?" Her turn to eye the ceiling for emphasis.

"I've forgotten nothing. Especially those who trespassed against me. Which is why I'm not bothered that Heaven, and my nephew, want to use my company to build up their army."

"You'd be okay with me having a baby angel?" she retorted.

"Who says it would be angelic? Where do you think imps come from?" He winked.

"Are you saying you want me to date Michael?"

"No, I want you to fuck Michael."

Her lips pursed. "That's crude."

"Aren't you the one trying to keep emotion out of it?" the Devil purred. "I've been watching you, Ash. Acting all business. Are you sure that's what you want?"

"I don't know what you mean."

"I mean, maybe the reason you've not taken anyone to bed is because you do want something more than just a guy squirting his juice all over your cherry blossom. Why else be so picky?"

She opened her mouth to give him a list, only to wonder if he was right. Was she looking for something extra?

For some reason, she thought of Derrick. How he made her feel. What he couldn't give her.

Which then brought her mind around to Michael. Before the interruption, she could honestly say she'd enjoyed herself. He was nice to look at. And she had the Devil's endorsement.

"I'll go on that date with the angel, but no guarantees."

"Unless they're overprice and useless. You wouldn't believe how much money we make selling those."

"Enough to ignore the whining I imagine when you don't honor them."

His smile widened. "And to think they used to say that women didn't have a head for business. Did you know, some of my finest soldiers started life as human females?"

"Is this your way of asking me to work more directly for you? Because if that's the case, we're going to need to renegotiate that contract."

"Anytime you want to give me more, you let me know. Just about anything is negotiable, after all." She opened her mouth, but before she could say anything, the Devil added, "Except for the baby. On that, I won't budge."

Since the Devil insisted, she made the decision to meet the angel. She arrived five minutes early that night for her date with Michael, who was already at the restaurant, a place she'd never actually eaten at before. It was lovely, though, a five-star Michelin place that didn't take last-minute reservations. Yet she and Michael had a wonderful table set against a window that showed the busy street.

Yet for all the interesting things going on outside, Michael only had eyes for her.

She wished she could say the same. While he proved fascinating, her gaze kept straying, glancing most often at the pub across the road with its darkened windows. Not her type of place at all, so why couldn't she ignore it?

She tried shifting so her back was slightly turned towards it. It felt as if something poked her in the back, as if she were being—

"...watched."

"What?" Huh?" Distracted, she suddenly turned her attention from the window to Michael.

"I said you feel it too, the fact we're being watched."

"Who?" she asked, only to sigh. "Derrick."

"He's been eyeballing you since we sat down."

"You can see him?" She glanced at the darkened bar window, then at her date.

"And you can sense him. I should have known he was lying when he said there was nothing between you."

"There isn't," she hotly claimed, and yet that wasn't entirely true. She desired him, a heck of a lot more than she wanted Michael. Which was just great.

She finally had a guy in front of her that she would have accepted a week ago. But then Derrick came along, and now she wanted the one guy she shouldn't have.

"I'm going to be one hundred percent truthful with you. I'm not interested in a permanent romantic attachment. Like you, I have certain obligations."

"Don't tell me you're trying to make a baby, too?" The idea kind of tore at her. On the one hand, weren't angels supposed to be the embodiment of purity? On the other hand, hadn't their kind been seducing humans for centuries?

"We each have a duty to perform, but it doesn't have to be unpleasant."

Her lips pursed. "If this is your roundabout way of saying you give good sex, then I suggest you stop right now."

"More like saying we can give each other what's needed. No strings, as you humans say."

"You mean handle this like a business arrangement?" He suggested the very thing she'd been seeking, and yet it left her conflicted.

"Yes."

He was offering her an easy way out.

She felt the stare burning into her from across the road.

"Can I think about it?"

"Take all the time you need."

Their dinner and dessert finished, he escorted

her home, walking her to the front door before pausing.

They both heard the motorcycle that abruptly died. Derrick had followed, and still hadn't confronted.

Because he didn't care. She must have been misreading the signals. Or he'd decided that he wasn't interested anymore.

Which annoyed her. He was the one who'd started the flirting.

The one who'd gotten her hot and bothered and confused.

The reason she wasn't giving the perfect man in front of her a chance.

"Kiss me," she demanded.

"What?" Michael appeared startled by the request.

"Kiss me. You're right. We are perfect for each other. There's no reason to wait." She puckered and lifted her lips. Closed her eyes.

Waited.

Heard a grunt.

A scuff.

Felt a hot rush of air. Then silence.

Heat swirled around her, licking at her, cradling.

It wasn't Michael standing in front of her. She knew that without even having to open her eyes.

She knew it was Derrick.

Felt the flutter of his cloak surrounding her.

The hot puff of breath, his mouth close.

But not touching.

Was he waiting for an invitation?

She opened her eyes to see Derrick. But a Derrick like she'd never seen. There was a wildness in his gaze. Anger, too. But it was the confusion that truly struck her.

He wanted to kiss her. The passion in him was leashed, yet it strained, pulsed as if it needed to escape. The fact that he tried to control it only made it fiercer.

And she knew what ignited it.

Jealousy.

He desired her, and there was something heady about that knowledge.

This man. This virile, strong man. Wanted her.

She swayed towards him and cocked a half-smile. "Are you ever going to kiss me?" she dared.

"If you insist."

His mouth pressed intently. Her senses flared. Lit the spot between her legs. Made her desire ignite.

His hands cupped her ass and drew her hard against him, and she felt the clench between her thighs.

Touch me. She trembled at the hope that he'd cup her. Stroke her.

She moaned as he thrust his leg between hers,

and rubbed against her, bringing forth a heavy moan.

The sound had him drawing back, giving her an indecipherable expression that turned into a vehement, "Fuck me!" before Derrick flung himself away from her and literally stepped out of sight.

1 0

Fuck.

Fuck.

And fuck again.

He was supposed to keep his distance. Instead, he'd kissed her. Why had he done that?

Actually, for starters, why had he gotten rid of Michael?

Why did he care who Ash kissed?

He shouldn't, yet he'd flown into a rage when he saw her tilting her chin, asking that fucking angel for a kiss.

Like hell.

Jealousy proved more powerful than he'd ever expected. He couldn't stand and watch another man put his mouth on hers. So, he lost his cool and swept in. It was so easy to grab hold of the angel, summon a portal, and toss him in.

He'd no sooner gotten rid of the unwanted rival than he saw those lips. Perfect, anticipating. Waiting for another man, which meant he couldn't touch them.

Then she opened her eyes, only halfway, her expression sultry. And not surprised to see him. She'd known who was standing there.

Asked *him* for a kiss.

He should have said no. He couldn't get involved. Wouldn't.

Tell that to the madness coursing through his veins. Desire took over for a moment, and he claimed her mouth. Kissed her. Would have taken her right then and there. Instead, he walked away. Floated. Whatever. He took off, but the fire in him still raged.

"Why didn't I stay?" he cried while pacing his apartment.

"A good question. Why the fuck did you leave? My second-favorite witch was hot for you," Lucifer exclaimed. He stepped into the basement apartment, a baby, swaddled in pink, tucked against an arm.

"Dark Lord." His greeting was a hastily dipped knee.

"What is wrong with you? Since when do you

walk away from willing pussy? What the fuck is wrong with you, boy?"

"I—" He hesitated. "I panicked, my lord."

"Do ya think?" exclaimed the Devil, smoke pouring from his nose. The baby reached for it, and when her hands couldn't grasp it, her face screwed up in annoyance. Before she could yell, the Devil tossed the child into the air.

Before Derrick could shout, "Low ceiling!" the baby passed through as if a boundary didn't exist, her giggling getting fainter then turning to a happy, strident shriek as she fell back down and plopped into her daddy's arms. The uninjured child gurgled and smiled.

But the more frightening thing was seeing Lucifer's expression. Adoration, and a hint of sadness.

"Let me tell you something, Derrick. Daughters are the best and worst thing to happen to a man. They wrap you around their little finger when they are young. It's when they get older that they try to rip out your heart. It's why I keep mine in a safe place."

"I don't think I'll have a problem with daughters, Dark Lord, with my being sterile and all."

"So you keep reminding me. It's almost as if you'd like me to reverse what I did to you. And you know, I've been giving it some thought."

"What?" Derrick might have gaped stupidly as the words filtered into his brain.

"I thought about making your soldiers active again, but you were pretty adamant at the time. No kids. Which I can understand given what happened to yours. But then again, what did you expect? You were the number three man in a gang. Such a violent one, too. You had to expect what would happen to your family."

His lips flattened. The reminder that he couldn't save his wife and kid rankled. Thirty years might have passed since they were killed, but it still had the power to hurt. Which was why he'd made a specific deal with the Devil. "I made sure it wouldn't happen again."

"And that's where you went wrong. I've lost children, many of them over the centuries. Some more memorable than others. And despite how it always ends, I still make the mini-mes. I enjoy them despite all the puking and shitting and the attempts to kill me. Children keep you feeling young."

Derrick didn't disagree, although at the time when he had a son, he'd been so busy with the gang, he'd not paid him enough mind. Not kept them safe.

"Was there a reason you came to see me, my lord?"

"Attempting to change the subject. And not very subtly."

"You mocked me for not sleeping with your witch. Sorry to disappoint. Now, if we're done?"

"Actually, we're not because your lack of performance wasn't why I came. I am here because of a cock-blocking complaint. Apparently, you interfered on a Grim-arranged date."

"I did." Derrick told the truth, which probably wasn't in his favor.

The Devil tucked his hands behind his back, showing off the clean lines of his suit—he had a very high-end CEO appearance today. Not a duck in sight. "According to the complaint, you stole a kiss."

"I didn't steal it. She knew it was me and asked me for it."

"Consent wasn't in question, it's the fact that the only reason it happened was because you removed the client she was originally planning to embrace. Correct?"

"I don't think Michael is the right guy for Ashley." Problem being, Derrick wasn't the right guy either.

"If we follow the models we ran, based on the angel's questionnaire, and the witch's, they are eminently compatible."

"He doesn't care about her."

"No, but he was willing to fuck her and donate his soldiers to the cause until you interfered."

There were all kinds of lies Derrick could have

used to justify his actions. He stuck to the most popular one. "I was drunk."

"That's a poor excuse. And a lie. You weren't that wasted. You knew exactly what you were doing."

"You want me to say I was jealous, then fine. I didn't want that fucking angel touching her." The ugly truth.

"Ah, the truth, which I usually abhor, but in this case, your coveting pleases me. You didn't want to share. Totally understandable. I'm not a big proponent of it either. It's why I tend to break things before letting other people borrow them."

"I don't want to break Ashley."

"You just want to give her the meat sausage. I get it. Really, I do. But is that what's best for Ashley?" the Devil asked. "And more importantly, how does that help me?"

"How does letting an angel impregnate your handmaiden help you?" was Derrick's retort.

"As if the child would be angelic." Lucifer snorted, hot huffs of smoke emerging. "Have you met my witch? No way is a child of her loins getting past my brother's precious pearly gates."

"Oh."

"Yes, oh. You just ruined my chance to one-up Heaven. Michael knows he's supposed to demand a human as his potential baby-angel-making machine. But he asked for Ashley. And if he gave her a runt that didn't take after the oh-so-pure father, can you imagine the embarrassment? Their precious Michael, making imps for the Devil. It would be an in-your-face moment." The Devil smiled as he sighed, thinking of it.

"Perhaps if you'd explained this to me beforehand."

"Did you just fucking asking your Dark Lord to relay his plans to *you*?" For a moment, the Devil grew in size, a monstrous thing of pressure that had Derrick dipping his head and mumbling, "I'd never dare ask you, my king. Your will is my command."

The pressure eased. "I should bloody well hope so. Really, I expected better from you. I mean, first you cock block, and then you don't even follow through? How cruel is that? My poor second-favorite witch went from about to get laid, to lying horny and alone in her bed. Next time, mind your business and let her spread those lovely thighs of hers for a willing sausage that isn't shooting blanks." The Devil aimed some finger pistols and added sound effects. "Given you're getting in the way of that happening, you've been removed from her case."

"What? But—" He started to protest.

"No buts. My witch asked the company to find her someone to make a baby." Lucifer held up his daughter and made faces as he said, "And we will deliver on that promise."

"Don't make it Michael."

"Oh, for fuck's sake. You know we're setting her up with the angel. What part of in Heaven's face did you not get? And to make sure you don't interfere, the location of their next date will be a secret. If you don't let it happen, there will be consequences," the Devil stated.

"Understood." Derrick growled.

"You'd better because I can't have any more interference. We don't have much time to build our armies. The threat is coming, faster than expected."

"What threat?"

"Did I say threat?" Lucifer grinned. "Catch!"

A pink bundle flew, and Derrick only had a moment to catch the wriggly baby. He held it out from him as if she might explode.

The baby smiled and waved her arms.

"She's trying to hug you," Lucifer said.

"I don't—"

"You'd better not say no to my Jujube," was the warning.

A glance at the fading baby's smile meant that Derrick reeled her in close. It wasn't horrible. As a matter of fact, the warm, squishy child was kind of nice. And she smelled good.

She babbled and grabbed his cheeks, blew bubbles, and gurgled some more.

Lucifer cocked his head. "She likes you."

"Uh, thanks."

The baby grinned, only a single tooth jutting from her gum, and drool rolling off her chin. She belched, hard enough that he blinked and could have sworn he felt it.

"Good girl!" Lucifer exclaimed, scooping up his daughter. "Now do a poopy for Daddy before bedtime. A great big one that I can set on fire and put outside those gates." It was the last thing Derrick heard before the Devil popped out of sight.

With his apartment empty, and his buzz wearing off, there was nothing to do but sit in a chair, a bottle of whiskey in hand, and think about Ashley.

Who wasn't his problem anymore. He'd been taken off her case.

Told to stay away from the witch.

Screw what the Devil wanted. What about what he wanted? What about what Ashley deserved? She should be with someone who appreciated her.

Like me.

THE POUNDING at Ashley's door drew her from the living room, and she didn't need to check her video doorbell screen to know who it was.

Derrick.

The only man to make her aware in a way she'd never imagined. She placed her fingers on the door.

"Ashley." He murmured her name.

She didn't reply.

"I know you're behind this door."

One that would stay shut. She glanced at the runes she'd painted above it, blocking him from entering.

"Open up."

She went to walk away, but he whispered, "I am sorry I left you mid-kiss."

"Then why did you?" she couldn't help but blurt.

"Because I'm the wrong guy for you. I can't give you what you want."

"How do you know what I want?" She thought she'd known until that kiss. But now…

"I can't give you a child."

"Never asked you to. Or did you think I was stupid? That I didn't know what I was doing when I asked you to kiss me." He wasn't entirely wrong. Kissing Derrick wasn't about her deal with the Devil but what she wanted as a woman.

She wanted Derrick.

She palmed the door and would have sworn she felt his hands through it.

"Ash, I—"

She swung open the portal, and he almost fell inside. He recovered. "Let me—"

"Shut up and get in here." She grabbed him by the shirt and dragged him inside. Rising on tiptoe, she got her lips close enough to touch.

That was all it took to get swept away by the passion.

Once they started kissing, she couldn't stop herself. There was no sense in denying the pull she felt. Why fight it when giving in felt so good? He hugged her close and muttered against her lips.

"Are you sure about this?"

For a supposed badass biker and reaper, he was

awfully concerned about her feelings. "Shut up and kiss me."

"As my lady commands." He claimed her lips once more, coaxing them open, teasing her bottom lip while she tickled with the tip of her tongue.

He grunted when her hands slid from his back to cup his ass. Nice and firm.

He repaid the favor in kind, palming her cheeks, clasping her firmly against him.

Fire consumed her, and by the heat radiating from him, reciprocated. A slide of wet tongues did nothing but further stoke the passion. It was a wonder their clothes didn't burn. What she wouldn't give to feel his flesh against hers.

She tugged at his shirt, shoving it upwards and sliding her hands under. Skimming them over taut skin. He groaned but helped her free him from the fabric hiding him from her.

The sight of his body made her entire body tingle. Big. It was the only word to describe him; broad shoulders, thick with muscle, well-defined arms with biceps larger than both her hands. A wide chest with even more slabs of muscle. She ran a finger down his pecs, and he growled.

"Your turn."

She lifted her arms when he tugged on the hem of her shirt. When she would have reached behind to unhook her bra, he shook his head, only a corner of his lips lifting.

"Leave it on for a moment, would you? I want to take my time."

She arched a brow. "Take your time later. I want you now."

The statement surprised him. She saw it in the widening of his eyes, felt it in the urgent passion as he swept in for another kiss, the weight of him pushing her back against a wall. Her arms curled around his neck, and her leg rose to wrap around his hip. He dipped slightly, and the new angle meant he could grind himself against her, drawing gasps and moans.

"What is it about you that makes me lose control?" he murmured against her mouth.

She nipped his lip. "Don't overthink it." She didn't want him leaving again, not now with her blood boiling.

His hands were rough as they grabbed her pants and shoved them down. She kicked free of the trousers and rewrapped her leg around his waist. When his fingers clamped onto her ass and lifted, her other limb found its place, locking her against him. The core of her pressed against the bulging front of his pants.

With one arm wrapped around her, holding her aloft, he fumbled with his belt and the fly of his jeans. The sound of tearing fabric only making her hotter.

When he freed himself, the heated length of him sprang forward and slapped against her sex. He rubbed himself against her.

Teasing.

She wiggled impatiently in reply and nipped at his mouth again.

He answered with a growl and both his hands on her hips. He angled her until the tip of him parted her nether lips. He pressed in. Pushed into her snug and welcoming sheath. Her toes curled at the pleasure of it.

She gripped him tightly, her arms and legs wrapped, her mouth latching on to his neck. Sucking away. Tugging at the skin, feeling his rapidly beating pulse. For a dead man, he was more than alive.

He pumped her hard. He thrust fast. He slammed his cock in and out of her, finding just the right angle, the one that drew mewling cries. He knew the spot to hit. And he did so over and over again. The muscles of her sex gripped him tightly, and with each stroke into her sweet spot, she squeezed even more.

He was unrelenting, and soon, her fingers dug into his shoulders as her body coiled, about to come. When she finally tipped over the edge, she screamed.

He let out a yell of his own as he thrust one last time into her. Deep. Pulsing.

They trembled against each other. Their breath ragged. Their pleasure intense and slowly fading.

Even when she began to stir, he wouldn't let go. He cradled her close to him, his face buried in her hair. He kept her near as he carried her to bed, where he worshiped her body more slowly, this time. Letting his fingers explore and tease her flesh until she was parting her legs, panting for him to ease her ache.

She came again, harder even than the first time, and was so boneless and relaxed in his arms after, she fell asleep.

She woke warm and content, face cradled on his chest, her leg splayed over him. It was utter perfection, except for the urge to pee. It dragged her from bed to the bathroom, sitting half-asleep on the toilet, squinting by the glow of her nightlight at the toilet paper that had writing on it. Not just any writing, her contract with the Devil, and the last line of it a counter ticking down...

Time was running out. Either she got pregnant soon, or she'd be dead and dragged to Hell.

1 2

RATHER THAN COME BACK to bed after using the bath-room, Derrick heard Ash moving out of the bedroom. Rattling around in the kitchen. It was too early to be cooking. It was only five a.m.

Her anger could only mean one thing. She regretted what'd happened.

Fuck. He had to fix it. Could he even change her mind?

Only one way to find out. He slid on his jeans, left them unbuttoned but zipped. No shirt. Yeah, he was going to use the advantages he had.

He sauntered out. "Hey, beautiful. You making coffee?"

She eyed him through a hank of hair. Her lips pursed, but only for a moment. "I was going to make some breakfast. How do you feel about eggs and bacon?"

"Add in some toast, and you're a goddess."

Her lips twitched. "And if I said I might even throw in some hashbrowns?"

"I might just be in love." The word slipped from his lips. She gaped in shock. He might have, too. They both quickly turned and pretended that it didn't happen. Him looking for something to do with his hands, her banging around with the frying pan.

Why the fuck had he said that? What the hell was wrong with him?

Breakfast was slightly awkward at first, but as they ate and drank some coffee, they actually talked, this time about an upcoming Renaissance festival. The idea intrigued.

"You mean, people can dress up like knights and walk around openly with swords?" he queried.

"Yes. It's been going on for ages. You're not that old. Surely, you've heard of it."

He rolled his shoulders. "I never showed much interest in things outside the gang."

"Did you ever travel?"

"I went to a few places. Like Mexico once, on business."

She shook her head. "We should…" She paused,

bit her lip, and then restarted. "Maybe you'll let me show you some places sometime."

She hadn't rejected him. On the contrary, she wanted them to go out again.

"Tell me where you want to go first. We can leave right now."

"No, we can't. For one. I have things to do."

"Like? It's Saturday. You don't work."

"But I have things like laundry. And dusting."

He glanced around. "This place is immaculate."

"Exactly. Weekly cleanings are the reason why."

"I'll help you. Then we can be done early and go out."

She shook her head. "I'm not available tonight."

"Why not?"

"I have dinner plans with Michael."

He froze and stared at her. "What do you mean you have plans? After last night… Aren't we…?" He didn't know how to articulate everything he'd assumed.

"What you and I have is passionate. And fun. I want to do that again. More than you could know. But I still have an obligation. If I don't give the Devil what he demands, I'll be sent to Hell."

"It's not as bad as you think," he argued.

Not exactly the right answer judging by the tightening of her features.

"Maybe you're okay with it, but I'm not. You're

talking about sending me somewhere that needs constant dusting because of falling ash. I'd never be fully clean. I don't want to go to Hell. Not yet."

He could see why. Like him, she'd barely lived her life. But she had a chance to still enjoy it.

Meaning, she had to fulfill the terms of her contract.

"You need to fuck Michael." Saying it bluntly didn't make it any better.

She didn't wince but lifted her chin. "You can lose the attitude. You don't own me. I can do as I please."

"You're right. You can. Go ahead and do it, as often as you like," he snapped. "Go and make a baby with that sanctimonious prick. Go be a—" He cut himself off before he said something truly heinous.

But he didn't need to speak it for her eyes to widen, then narrow.

"Get out."

"Ash, I'm sorry. I—"

"I said. Get. Out." She put some force behind the words, and the air vibrated, coalescing around him to shove him towards the door.

"Come on, Ash. I'm sorry." He would have said more, maybe tried to explain the difficulty he was having with jealousy, but that magical force kept him moving right out the door. It slammed shut.

It didn't help that he heard the Devil behind him clap and say, "Bravo, that was an excellent way to make sure you burned your bridge with the witch. You got what you wanted, some hot pussy for a single night and got away, without even a scratch. Congratulations."

The Devil's glee only made the angst churning in him worse.

What have I done?

Pushed her into the arms of another.

13

Hours later, and she still wanted to hunt Derrick down and shake him.

Then kiss him because as angry as his actions made her, she understood why he'd been that way.

Jealousy. Pure and simple. He couldn't bear the thought of her with another man. She got it. Really, she did. Because the idea of him with another woman? She probably wouldn't have taken it very well.

However, did appeasing his jealousy mean more than the prospect of going to Hell?

Sorry, Derrick. She'd meant what she said. *I own myself.* She wasn't about to gamble her future on a guy she'd just met. Yes, the sex was good. Yes, he made her feel incredible. But...what if it lasted a week? A month? What if she went to Hell, and he stayed on Earth?

She had no idea what the future would bring. Would she really wager it on one man?

The turmoil in her head led to a frenzy of cleaning. Feather dusting everything. Vacuuming. Scrubbing. She could have licked her floor by the time she was done. She didn't feel any calmer.

It didn't help that he'd not tried to call or knock on her door. Maybe he'd already moved on.

In that case, good thing she had a date. The longer her phone went without ringing, her text not pinging, and her door not being banged on, the more she simmered.

Had he used her? He obviously didn't like Michael. Could sleeping with her have been a ploy to one-up the angel?

She'd hate to think herself so gullible and yet, what if she'd misread him?

Could be the sex meant nothing to him, in which case, she worried over nothing. It meant she didn't have to feel any guilt for keeping her date with Michael.

She still had a baby to make and an appointment with Hell to delay.

She dressed with care, wearing a wraparound dress with easy access. If she could get the business done in an alley or a car somewhere, then she could just go home after, have a nice cup of cocoa, and immerse herself in a book.

Even her mind winced at her callous regard. Could she really be that cold?

Did she want to die and be stuck in Hell?

It wasn't as if the angel were a horrible person. Seeing Michael again, she was reminded of how handsome and courteous he could be. He said all the right things. Acted perfectly. In just about every respect, he ticked all the boxes.

But he left her colder than a witch's tit in a church during a sermon.

I don't think I can do this. The realization hit her during dessert, which meant that when Michael offered a suave smile and said, "Shall we go somewhere private to continue our evening?" she froze.

"Ashley. Did you hear me? I asked—"

She shook her head. "I heard you. It's just…" She trailed off. How to say that she found him very attractive, but she couldn't sleep with him?

"Is something wrong? You seem off this evening."

She bit her lip rather than say anything. "I'm sorry." She took a deep breath and decided to tell him the truth. Or a partial version of it anyway. "I might have accidentally gotten involved with someone."

"Accidentally?" He arched a brow at her choice of words. "How does that happen?"

Somehow, claiming she'd fallen on his dick didn't seem right. "It kind of happened, and it's probably not going anywhere. Actually, I know it isn't," she added in a low mutter. Which was one mutter too many.

"Derrick." Michael stated his name, lips curved in amusement. "I take it he didn't stop at a kiss."

Her cheeks flushed. "It didn't, which is why I feel like I have to say something."

"I appreciate your honesty. Even as I'm surprised by your choice. You must really care for him, given he can't give you what you need to save your soul."

She blinked at him. "You know about my deal with Lucifer?"

"Did you think I chose you by mere chance?"

The statement silenced her for a moment. She couldn't really be angry that he'd been calculating rather than impassioned when it came to her. She'd been doing the same thing. Looking for the perfect specimen to satisfy a need. Yet she couldn't help but compare how he made her feel to the attraction she felt for Derrick.

From the first moment, she'd been drawn by the reaper's appearance. Yes, he made her angry, but he also engaged her senses. Made her wish things were different.

But she couldn't ignore reality. And Derrick

wasn't here. Michael sat, waiting patiently. Willing to give her what her contract demanded.

Turning him down was stupid. "We could go to my place," she found herself saying.

"That sounds fantastic."

Really? Then why did she feel as if every step she took dragged?

In short order, they were on the street, and she didn't know what she expected. Maybe that Michael would pop some wings and fly them or conjure them a ride on a fluffy cloud. Instead, he asked, "Where did you park?"

"I didn't drive."

"Did you ride in on a broom?" He asked it in all seriousness, and she gaped in disbelief.

"You did not just ask me that."

"Why are you looking angry? It's a valid question. You're a witch."

"I don't ride a broom. Never have."

"Then how are we supposed to get to your house?"

"If you're trying to be funny, you're failing." She couldn't help but give him a stern glare.

"You should try smiling more often. You're much prettier that way." Absolutely the wrong thing for him to say.

"I'm going to walk. By myself." She stepped away from Michael, who appeared confused.

"If I'm not accompanying you, how will I get there?"

"You won't. Because I am uninviting you."

The bemusement turned to annoyance. "You can't do that."

"I can. And did. I've no interest in you."

"What are you talking about? How can you not be interested?" He looked genuinely flummoxed. "We are perfectly compatible."

"Maybe on paper, but in person, you're barely okay."

"Let me guess, the reaper is more than okay." Michael sneered.

"Derrick is the best," said by the man himself as he stepped out of a shadow. Derrick joined them, wearing his usual battered leather coat and molded jeans. But he swayed on his feet, the reek of alcohol another indication that he was stinking drunk.

Wait? Had he been imbibing and moping this entire time?

"Not you again. You were told to not interfere," Michael snapped.

Derrick smirked. "Yeah, well, you know what they say: rules are made to be broken. How do you think I ended up working for the Devil?"

"Why are you here?" she asked.

"Why do you think?" He straightened, and his

expression somewhat cleared. "I don't want you to be with another guy. I want you to be with me."

It was the thing she'd wanted to hear all day.

Michael uttered a rude chuckle. "Listen to the lies."

"What lie? I want her," Derrick exclaimed.

"And in your selfish need to beat me, will condemn her to Hell!"

Derrick's expression fell, and she could see why he'd needed the alcohol to have the courage to say anything.

Which was why she said, "My relationship with Derrick is none of your business."

That drew an icy glare. "You would choose this belligerent excuse of a male over me?"

"Yes." Perhaps she'd live to regret it, but in her heart, she wanted Derrick to be the only man in her bed.

Apparently, angels didn't handle rejection well. Michael got an ugly expression on his face. His wings snapped out, and they weren't the pretty fluffy things she expected. He flicked one, and she cried out as it clipped her.

It didn't hurt her. More like it surprised, but Derrick went ballistic.

"Fucking asshole. Don't you dare touch her!" Derrick dove and swung at Michael. The angel ducked, and Derrick tried a sloppy counter that opened him up for the well-placed fist Michael launched.

Derrick hit the ground hard and lay there for a second. Stunned.

Rather than give him a moment to recover, Michael moved in, foot winding back for a kick.

She almost interfered, but in that half-second of slow-moving time, as she made her decision, Derrick's gaze met hers, hot and possessive.

Her lips parted.

He winked. And suddenly, that foot went through nothing as a shadow suddenly exploded from Derrick's back. His cloak covered him, head to toe, a dark, undulating thing that Michael's foot passed through.

The black, amorphous fabric coalesced back into a man. All signs of inebriation disappeared. His gaze steadied. His expression grim.

"You would dare fight me, reaper?" Michael boomed, glowing with a radiance that burned the eyes.

"I would die again just to smack that smug expression from your face. So, bring it." Derrick lifted his fists, and the pair began to spar, exchanging meaty thuds and grunts.

Ashley was transfixed. If she'd thought Derrick sexy before, it had increased exponentially with his dark cloak, snapping and waving around him, his expression grim and terrible. A sexy, dangerous, badass reaper, fighting for *her*.

Then there was Michael, his complete glowing opposite.

Apparently, she truly was the Dark Lord's hand-maiden because she knew which one she wanted.

The men thrust themselves apart, and Derrick half-crouched, fists at the ready.

But Michael stood tall and began to shine, bright enough to make her squint. While he wore no halo, he pulled a glowing sword from a sheath strapped to his leg.

"Isn't it just like an angel to bring a big knife to a fight?" Derrick taunted.

"You are boring me. Let us finish this."

"If you insist." Derrick held out his hand, and silver-hued baseball bat appeared, complete with barbed wire and spikes.

At the sight of it, Michael arched a brow. "What is that?"

Whereas she chuckled as she murmured, "Someone hasn't been keeping up with *The Walking Dead*."

"Batter up!" Derrick swung the weapon from side to side, and it occurred to her that she should stop the fight. They would cause serious damage.

Before she could say a word, the Devil whispered in her ear. "Don't you dare. I wanna watch."

Even if she'd wanted to, she could say nothing. It was as if she were gagged. She glared sideways to see the Devil wearing red and blue 3D glasses, with a huge tub of popcorn avidly watching Derrick and Michael circling each other.

The angel sounded bored as he said, "Are you really going to fight me over a female?"

"Her name is Ashely."

"Her name doesn't matter. Her only use was as a womb for me to plant my seed."

The Devil cackled. "Wow, that's truthful even for one of those fuckers."

She growled. "This isn't funny. My life is not your entertainment."

"On the contrary, it is. This is better than any soap opera."

"You do realize someone might get hurt."

"No mights about it," said a gleeful Devil. "Someone will definitely get hurt."

"You could stop this," she said as the two men circled each other, being more cautious now that the weapons were out.

"I could," agreed the Devil. "But I won't. After all, the winner will fuck you. I think only the strongest should be the father of your child. Don't you?"

"If I had a choice, it would be Derrick," she snapped. "And you know it."

"Derrick, eh? But he can't give you offspring."

"I don't care." In that moment, she really didn't. "I'd rather go to Hell than create a child with someone other than Derrick." A choice she might regret later, but at the same time, she already knew that she'd end up in Hell. It would just be sooner than expected.

"Then I guess you better hope he wins."

14

DERRICK HAD SPENT the day getting drunk after the fight with Ashley. Spent all day convincing himself that it was better this way. He knew what would happen if he started caring, His enemies would target her just as they'd targeted his wife and child back when he ran with the gang.

If he wanted proof, he only had to look at how Michael had gone after her.

So many reasons to walk away, and yet, he found himself pacing outside her place. Waiting for her to return from her date, a bottle of alcoholic reinforcement in hand—the hellish kind that made even a reaper drunk.

A part of him clamored about the desperation he showed. He drank to silence it. Yes, he was a little desperate. The first woman to make him care since his failure as a father and husband was on a date with another man.

One doing his utmost to fuck her.

He took a long swig and drained the bottle. Tossed it when it had nothing left.

He found himself wandering the street. Where was she? Still at dinner? What if they'd gone back to Michael's place? A hotel? Maybe even the nearest alley…

Where is she?

He felt it then, that tug that used to let him know a soul clamored for his attention. He didn't question, simply followed, not surprised at all when he emerged to find Ash with her date.

With the alcohol making his choices poor, he attacked. Failed miserably and found himself flat on the ground. Where he might have stayed if he'd not seen her face.

Ash appeared stricken as she reached for him. Not her hand. Her soul. In that moment, he realized something.

She loves me.

He couldn't let her see him like this. Nor would he let a mere angel make a fool of him. He drew on his robe, and the drunken haze disappeared. He saw the world quite clearly, especially the enemy in front of him.

The angel thought he could take Derrick's woman from him?

Like fuck.

"You know you can't win against me. This sword has been blessed." Mike waved his glowing toy.

"And?" Derrick taunted. He'd never fought an angel before, and vaguely recalled a rule against it. As if that would stop him.

"I'll show you what it means to defy God."

The blade flashed towards him, and Derrick blocked it with his bat.

Clang.

"You'll have to do better than that," he taunted. Jabbing playfully with his weapon.

The angel slapped it aside. They sparred for a few strokes before Michael suddenly staggered, and Derrick wound up for a swing, missing the dagger suddenly in Michael's other hand.

He gasped as it sliced through an undulating wave of his cloak, severing it. He staggered. His cloak waved erratically, no longer fully obeying his commands.

Michael smiled. "Did no one ever tell you blessed weapons cut through your dark magic? Give up, reaper, and you'll live."

"No."

"She's just a woman."

"A woman I care for. You don't."

"What's caring have to do with sex?" asked Michael, genuinely baffled.

"Everything," growled Derrick as he threw himself at the angel. The next few moments were a blur of movement, feet sliding and dancing to stay out of arm's reach, blades and his bat flashing as they wove a pattern that resulted in metallic rings as each blow was blocked.

However, in one thing, Michael was right. He would win. Derrick could fight, but he was young compared to Michael, and apparently a rookie in terms of experience.

The angel whittled at him, carving at his cloak, weakening him, wounding him enough that he couldn't fog to absorb the blows.

When Michael surprised him by rushing close and smashing the pommel of his dagger against his jaw, he heard Ash cry out.

He couldn't help but glance at her, thus missing the kick. He blinked at the ground, head and eyes ringing, feeling frail and human, afraid too. Because the last time he'd been face down, he'd died from a bullet to the head.

Apparently, he was doomed to repeat his mistakes. Once more, he didn't manage to save the woman he loved.

Instead, she saved him. She threw herself in front

of the angel, a hand held up in a stopping gesture. "Back the fuck up!" she snapped.

"Out of the way, witch, while I finish him off. And then we shall discuss your behavior."

"I don't think so." And then she did the one thing no human or witch should ever do.

She kicked an angel in the balls.

15

THE DEVIL TRIED to warn her, "Don't get involved."

Yet when Derrick reeled, and then fell because of her, she leaped to save him. He didn't deserve to die because she'd been too stupid to realize that she was doing the wrong thing.

She put herself between them, one small woman between an angel and a reaper. And when that so-called holy warrior pissed her off, she went old school.

He folded with a gasp, but not for long. She should have known better, given his less-than-impressively-sized hands and feet.

Michael recovered quickly, his blades held out at his sides, his expression icy. "You shouldn't have done that."

"And you should have listened when I said I wasn't interested in you."

"Are you sure you wish to choose him over me?"

"I'd choose the Devil himself over you." Said with a tilt of her chin.

"Let me hasten your descent to Hell then." It was a threat he acted on immediately.

The sword went through her stomach, like a knife through butter, except the soft, squishy shit was her guts.

The glowing blade withdrew without a sound. She didn't cry out as she slumped. She was much too surprised. She should have been panicking at her imminent death, and yet she found herself oddly unafraid. Hell was just the next stage of her existence.

"Bastard!" Derrick recovered enough to catch her before she could smack her face off the pavement. She wanted to warn him to watch for treachery, but the angel was done. He took off with a mighty beat of his wings. He'd done all the damage he needed to do.

Derrick cradled her, his expression anguished. "Don't die."

"I don't think I have a choice." She breathed in, and it hurt. So much.

"I'll get you to a hospital."

With trembling fingers, she cupped Derrick's cheek. "It's too late."

"Our Dark Lord, who art in fucking Hell, do something," he bellowed. "Lucifer, damn you, answer me."

"Did you just yell for me? Because you know I do so love it when my minions think they can order me the fuck around," the Devil replied.

Derrick turned from her to address him. "Save her."

Lucifer strolled over and cast a shadow on her. "Why would I do that? If she dies and goes to Hell, then you can visit her anytime. As a former employee of mine, I'll put her somewhere in the third circle. That's where I put my favorite damned souls."

"I don't want her to die, though," Derrick growled.

"Well, I'm kind of bound, you know. By her contract. You can't expect me to reward her, after all. She hasn't fulfilled her terms of the bargain."

"If you let her live—"

The Devil cut him off. "Don't even go there. We both know even if she'd not gotten gutted, I wasn't getting a baby. She's obviously in love with you, and you made it very clear you don't want any."

He'd made that demand when his pain was fresh.

Derrick's lips pressed. "What if I said I'd changed my mind?"

"Don't," she whispered. The Devil had told Ashely Derrick's story while he fought Michael. She understood why he was sterile. Knew what he'd lost and why he didn't want to suffer that pain again. She clung to his hand and squeezed. "I'm not afraid to die."

"Yeah, well, I'm not ready for it." Derrick stood. "Dark Lord, I'd like to request a change to my terms."

"Are you sure?" Lucifer said, the flames in his eyes growing to take over the entire orb.

Derrick nodded.

The fire in the Devil's gaze burst free and consumed her, encasing her in intense heat that stole all the air, all sound, all her senses.

When she regained consciousness, she found herself being held in Derrick's arms.

He stared at her, saying nothing.

She had something to say. "Idiot."

"Hello to you, too," he rumbled.

"Why did you do that? I was ready to die for you."

"I know."

"This will only delay the fact that I'm going to Hell someday."

"Yeah, yeah, I know, and we'll deal with that when the time comes. But first…what do you say we give life together a shot?"

"Meaning, what exactly?"

"Me. You. A house. A dog. Kids."

"Sounds domestic."

"It is. And you deserve a chance to have it."

"What if I'm not the housewife and mommy type?"

"Then, we'll figure it out together."

"Fucking gag me already." Lucifer literally made noises.

"Leave, if you don't like it." She didn't take her gaze from Derrick.

"I'll leave, but mostly because it's date night. I'm finally going to get some. Or else." The Devil glowered.

"Speaking of getting some…" She winked. Whatever the Devil had done had left her feeling energized. And hungry.

Derrick grimaced. "We'll have to walk. I can't call a portal. My cloak…" It lay in a shredded ruin around him.

"Fucking angels and their fucking holy weapons. You just had to challenge one," grumbled the Devil. A snap of his fingers, and the cloak repaired itself, lengthening and spreading until the shadow of it undulated around Derrick's feet.

"Run along now, children. And thanks for fulfilling the terms of your contract."

"Are you getting old, Lucifer? The deed hasn't been done yet. But rest assured, we'll be giving it our best shot," Ashley couldn't help but sass as Derrick covered her with his cloak, hiding her nudity. Being reborn in Hell's fire had done a number on her clothes.

"You can try as much as you like. Or not. Up to you since Derrick hit the bullseye the first time."

"What?" Derrick exclaimed, mirroring her thought.

"Did you really think I was going to let the chance slip by to have my second-favorite witch get pregnant by my ninth-favorite reaper?"

"But I only just gave you permission," Derrick sputtered.

The Devil snickered. "As if I've ever waited for that before. Congrats."

The news was enough to snap her mouth shut. As for Derrick, he looked shell-shocked. He eyed her belly, then her face.

"I never meant to…I'm, uh…"

"Don't you dare apologize." She cupped his cheek. "This was how it should be."

"But the Devil. The child…"

"Don't worry about that. Worry about me."

"What's wrong? I thought he healed you. Are you still hurting?" Immediately, he ran his hands over her, looking for injury. Finding none.

"Can you get us to my house? Quickly." She clung to him, imbuing her demand with urgency.

The rip he sketched deposited them right into her living room. Private and perfect.

She dragged him close and kissed him. The idiot still thought something was wrong.

"Where?" Kiss. "Does it?" Smooch. "Hurt?"

She grabbed his hand and placed it against her mound.

"Oh." He cupped her, and this time when he kissed her, he took his time, slipping a tongue between her lips even as his finger parted her nether lips to stroke.

She arched into his touch, her hips tilting to give him access.

But he pulled away.

She pouted and complained. "Where are you going?"

"Bed. Now." He pointed to her bedroom door, and she smiled.

"First one there gets to be on top."

He slid past her, naked and ready, his cock a beautiful, jutting mast.

She shoved at him, his balance off, putting him on the bed.

"I thought I got to be on top."

She straddled his legs. "I lied. I want to play first." She placed her hand on his chest and lightly rubbed, exploring his smooth skin, her fingers skimming over one of his flat nipples. A fine tremor went through him. She pinched the bud, and he sucked in a breath.

"On your back," she ordered. "Get fully on the bed."

He moved, and she followed. When he stopped, she straddled his thighs and grabbed hold of him. Stroked him. Rubbed her thumb over that pearl at the top. Then tugged. Up. Down. She stroked, and he groaned.

"You need to stop."

"What if I don't want to?"

"I'm not coming all over your hand," he exclaimed before rolling her onto her back. His body covered hers, a welcome, heavy weight, his lips sought hers for a torrid kiss that she met with passionate delight.

Their tongues joined in a sinuous, wet dance that she felt between her legs. She wiggled and arched against him, but he wouldn't give her what she wanted. His cock was trapped between their bodies, a hard, throbbing length that she wanted.

She reached between them to grab hold of him, but he caught her hand, first one, then the other. He pulled them over her head, trapping them. She squirmed. But he didn't let go. She didn't want him to. His kiss was possessive but short-lived.

He slid his mouth across her jaw and down her neckline and didn't stop until his lips found her nipple. He tugged on it. Teased it. Sucked it. She writhed and moaned. Her hands trapped. She wanted to touch him.

But he kept teasing her. His hot mouth toying with her breasts, his thigh between her legs, rubbing against her.

"Derrick," she moaned, and he finally released her hands, but only so he could hold himself aloft over her, the tip of him probing. His erection rubbed against her sex, and she gasped.

"Say it," he murmured against her mouth.

"Say what? I want you."

He shuddered.

"I need you."

He began pushing into her.

Only when he was fully seated, did she whisper, "I love you."

A tremor went through him, and he stilled. Then turned wild. He began moving inside her, deep, long strokes that swirled and teased her. Pleased her.

Had her arching and moaning as she clung to his broad back. She dug her nails in as he pumped her, driving his slick length in and out. Rousing her passion. Feeding her need.

She opened herself to him, her legs spread wide. He went deep. Thrusting and pounding against her sweet spot, over and over, jolting her with intense pleasure, building into a pressure that had her mouth opening wide.

When she finally came, she erupted with a scream, her climax an explosion that shorted out all her senses and dragged him with her. He grunted, and his body went rigid. She felt the hot pulse inside her as he found his release. Not that it mattered anymore.

She'd not had sex with him the first time to get pregnant. And she'd not needed to have sex with him this time for anything other than pleasure.

And love.

This prim and proper witch had finally been swept off her feet.

EPILOGUE

"You left your sock on the floor!" Ash hissed, her eyes flashing. She held it up with one finger.

He smiled, the lazy kind that drove her nuts. "I did. I also put my bowl on the counter instead of inside the dishwasher."

"You're doing it on purpose!" she accused.

"I am. You're the one who complained you had too much energy. Just trying to help." While pregnancy made some women tired, Ashley couldn't stand to sit still.

Her lips morphed into a pout. "I've got nothing left to clean."

"Good thing I have a plan." He crooked a finger. "Come here, Ash."

"Why?"

His smile stretched even wider. "Because I'm

156

going to make you so dirty, you'll need a shower."

"Promise?" was her husky reply.

In public, she might be a neat freak who drove people nuts, but between the sheets, she was wanton, wild, and filthy. Especially those things she did with her mouth.

And since they'd talked to a lawyer, they'd both been feeling much better about the whole baby thing. Turned out when Lucifer said she owed him a baby, it only meant having one. They weren't actually expected to hand the child over.

Although Ashley had mused aloud, "Maybe we should occasionally drop the baby off at the Dark Lord's castle."

"Why the fuck would we do that?"

"I can think of a few reasons," she said.

All of them dirty.

ACROSS TOWN, IN THE POLICE PRECINCT...

Courtney barely had any time to read through the details of the case. Her newest client had already been in jail for too long. Hopefully, he knew to keep his mouth shut.

If not, she'd get whatever he confessed to tossed out. This wasn't her first criminal case.

And her client looked as expected: scruffy-jawed,

dressed in the prison's colors. And given that he had been accused of murder, handcuffed and tethered to the table bolted in the interview room. A loftier title than the bland gray space deserved.

He appeared bored and barely registered her presence as she entered, choosing instead to look past her.

He finally addressed her when the door closed. "Where's my lawyer?"

"I'm your lawyer."

He eyed her up and down. She knew what he saw, someone who probably didn't even reach his chin, young-looking for her age—meaning she knew what he'd likely say next.

"Yeah, you're not going to work," Dwayne drawled.

Which was why she let him spend the night in jail.

Not quite the end...

Ready for the next one? In Contempt of Kourtney, a lawyer for Hell has to defend a reaper accused of murder. Will they unravel the case in time to explore the passion simmering between them?

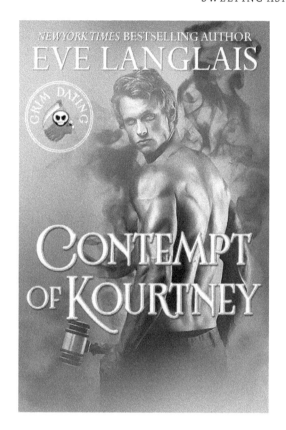

For more stories please see http://www.EveLanglais.com

Newsletter: http://evelanglais.com/newrelease

CPSIA information can be obtained
at www.ICGtesting.com
Printed in the USA
LVHW111624030621
689278LV00007B/1181